THE FOX

Clan Ross of the Hebrides

Pink Door Publishing

Print Edition

ISBN: 978-1-939356-94-9

A Note from the Author

In 1560, Scotland formally declared its split with the Catholic Church. John Knox, the leader of the Presbyterian movement banned the celebration of Christmas in Scotland from 1580 until about 1640.

Therefore, Clan Ross will be celebrating Hogmanay, a celebration of the new year, which consisted of days of games, gifts, and feasting.

One of the main traditions was "first footing" where a dark-haired man stepped over the threshold with shortbread, coal, black bun, and a wee dram of whiskey. In British and Manx folklore, the first foot is the first person to enter the home of a household on New Year's Day and is seen as a bringer of good fortune for the coming year.

Clan Ross of the Hebrides

This fictional story takes place at the beginning of the 17th century in the Scottish Hebrides, isles off the Isle of Skye's western coasts.

In the 1500s, lordship over the Hebrides collapsed and the power was given to clan chiefs. The MacNeil, in Barra, The Macdonald (Clanranald), in South Uist, The Uisdein, in North Uist and the MacLeod, the isles of Harris and Lewis.

For this series, I have moved the clans around a bit to help the story work better. The clans' locations in my books are as follows. The MacNeil will remain in Barra, The Macdonald (Clanranald) is moved to North Uist, The Uisdein resides in Benbecula, and the MacLeod remains in the Isles of Harris and Lewis. My fictional clan, Clan Ross, will laird over South Uist.

Also By Hildie McQueen

Clan Ross of the Hebrides

The Lion: Darach

The Beast: Duncan

The Eagle: Stuart

The Fox: Caelan

The Stag: Artair

The Hunter: Ella

Clan Ross Series

A Heartless Laird

A Hardened Warrior

A Hellish Highlander

A Flawed Scotsman

A Fearless Rebel

A Fierce Archer

Moriag Series

Beauty and the Highlander

The Lass and the Laird

Lady and the Scot

The Laird's Daughter

PROLOGUE

Ross Keep, South Uist Hebrides, Scotland
1603

"INTERESTING THAT SUDDENLY all my brothers are settling down," Caelan told his stepmother, Lady Mariel. "I will not fall into such a trap."

His stepmother chuckled. "I assure ye it is not a trap. I hope that when ye finally fall in love, it will not feel like one."

They sat in the parlor at Keep Ross. He'd arrived that evening as his stepmother had asked him to take her to visit his half brother, Stuart, and Stuart's wife, Cait, who lived on the west side of the isle in a place called *Eilean Daes*.

His eldest half brother and laird, Darach, would not leave the keep until his wife, Isobel, was fully recovered from childbirth.

His other half brothers also could not leave their duties. Ewan was busy preparing his lands for winter, Gideon had traveled to the southern guard post, and Duncan's wife, Beatrice, was about to give birth. That left him to help with what needed to be done when it came to his stepmother.

He didn't begrudge having to travel. In actuality, he looked forward to seeing his half brother and visiting the village now that it was fully rebuilt.

Although he'd never admit it to them, he missed Stuart

terribly and his cousin, Artair, who remained at *Eilean Daes*, and he looked forward to spending time with them.

"When do ye wish to leave?" Caelan asked, drinking the last of the tea in his cup. "Early in the morning?"

"That would be perfect," his stepmother replied, eyes bright with excitement. "Oh, did I mention we have another person traveling with us?"

Caelan let out a breath. "No, ye had not. Who?"

Just then a young woman walked in. Her clear green gaze barely hesitated on him before she looked to his stepmother and smiled widely. "I am sorry Aunt; I did not know ye had company."

"Nonsense," Lady Mariel said motioning to Caelan. "This is my stepson, Caelan. He is to take us to visit Stuart and Cait."

"Oh." The woman looked back to him. "I do not believe we have met."

His stepmother placed a hand on his forearm. "I do not suppose ye have. When Glynis visited last, ye were gone to the lowlands."

At the words, the woman studied him. "Ah, yes, now I remember. Ye are the brother who is more English than Scot."

The words made Caelan want to glare at her. Instead, he gave her a bland smile. "Is it more Scottish than English to state things one knows nothing of upon meeting someone for the first time?"

Her eyes widened and she glanced to his stepmother. "I do not know why I said that. Father always says I have the worst habit of blurting things without thought." She looked back to Caelan. "Please forgive me."

When she lowered her gaze, Caelan studied her. Whoever

she was she had to be the most enticing woman he'd ever laid eyes on. Her plump lips begging for a lingering kiss. Her round curves an invitation to pleasure. Her breasts—

"Caelan?" His stepmother gave him a curious look. "Accept Glynis's apology."

His lips curved. "Of course. It is forgotten"

Satisfied, his stepmother smiled. "Glynis is my niece and is visiting from Bara."

"Ah, a MacNeil," Caelan said as Glynis lowered to sit.

"Ye say it as if ye do not care for my clan," Glynis replied.

Caelan did not reply because if he were to be honest, there was one MacNeil he definitely did not care for. A young man at his school in Glasgow that he'd never gotten along with. But it was not something that mattered any longer.

"We leave early in the morning." He stood and walked from the room, unwilling to look and see how the woman was probably assessing his choice of clothing.

He was well aware he dressed much more English than Scottish.

CHAPTER ONE

MOUNTED ON HIS huge warhorse, Caelan and several guards surrounded the carriage that his stepmother, her companion Ana, and Glynis MacNeil traveled in. Feminine voices and laughter floated from the carriage, making the guards who rode alongside turn a time or two toward it.

Interesting how the presence of the fairer sex made the men sit straighter in the saddle and be more alert than usual to ensure their safety. Not to say that the men were not always doing their best, but even he would never allow any harm to come to the women.

His conversation with his stepmother the day prior came to mind. He'd not sought to court a woman before. It wasn't that he was against marriage, but more that he'd never met someone who he could see himself tied to for life.

There was also the fact that he was born out of wedlock. Not exactly a pedigree that would attract a highborn woman. Or most women for that matter.

With this woman, he'd instantly been attracted. Glynis was striking with her fair complexion, red hair, and the clearest green eyes he'd ever seen.

One of the forward guards held up a fist and everyone brought their steeds to a stop and went silent.

Caelan leaned down to the carriage window. "Be silent.

There is a party ahead and we are ensuring they are not a danger."

The three sets of eyes locked to him, but the only ones he noticed were the green ones.

"'Tis a pair of peddlers," a guard called out. "No threat."

Overhearing the guard, his stepmother's eyes widened as she looked to the other women.

She held out her hands making a motion for him to move. "Ask the peddlers to stop at once!" she ordered.

When he stared at her, she pointed to the carriage door. "Help us out, son."

"We cannot linger," Caelan said frowning toward the guard who galloped away to speak to the peddlers. "As it is, Stepmother, we will be hard-pressed to arrive before nightfall."

Promptly ignoring him, the women climbed out of the carriage and hurried in the direction of the waiting peddlers.

Excited at their good fortune, the sellers greeted the women with great enthusiasm.

Caelan motioned to a guard. "Remain with the carriage. The rest of ye, surround the peddlers and ensure no one else is about."

As the eight men did as they were told, he urged his mount ahead in order to patrol the area. It was on this same route that Stuart and Artair had been attacked just months earlier. Unlike that day, the sky was clear, and it was easy to see there were no threats.

As of late, South Uist had become more dangerous. People who traveled through the isle were often men escaping persecution from mainland Scotland for crimes.

Not only that, but with the late laird's passing things

changed. Darach ensured laws were enforced to protect the clan's people. There were those who were angry that they had lost control and the ability to gain from others' misfortune.

A guard returned from scouting ahead and gave him a curious look. "Why did ye stop?"

Caelan shrugged. "We came upon peddlers and the women demanded to shop for trinkets."

The man let out a bark of laughter. "Aye, women do love to acquire what they can from the traveling tempters."

"That is a good name for them," Caelan replied scanning the area. "Anything of note?"

The scout shook his head. "There is a group camped up ahead. Four in total, two men and two women. They are headed to the west shore and are not in any hurry. Actually, seem to be enjoying themselves.

"My stepmother will want to stop and speak to them," Caelan said looking up at the sky. "At this rate, we will not arrive until morning."

TRUE TO FORM, Lady Mariel insisted they stop upon spotting the people, who were now surrounding a small fire. Caelan argued that it was growing dark, and they would not arrive until well after dark. However, she insisted.

"My aunt, like my mother, has always had a heart for people," Glynis said standing next to him as he watched over his stepmother. "Ye should be proud of her. Not perturbed."

Blowing out an annoyed breath, he glanced down at her. "Ye seem to find it easy to make presumptions about my person."

"Ye look rather annoyed at her stopping to ensure the

people are well."

"Those people are not in harm's way. Therefore, the fact that we are losing daylight and must travel in the dark, which makes it dangerous for the horses, does annoy me."

"Here she comes now," Glynis said walking toward his stepmother, who smiled.

"I tried to convince them to travel with us to keep from any harm, but they insisted they wanted to remain there since it will be dark soon."

Caelan gave his stepmother a droll look. "Because Stepmother, traveling in the dark is dangerous."

When she came closer and cupped his jaw with her hand, his heart melted. "I am not afraid because ye are the bravest warrior I know and will keep us all safe."

At the words, Glynis grinned at him, eyes twinkling with mirth. Caelan narrowed his, but decided it was best not to say anything further.

His English appearance had lulled many an attacker to thinking him easy prey. However, those who knew him would think twice before confronting him. With sword in hand and temper loosed, he became someone else. A berserker of sorts.

In battle, he rarely was injured, nor did he ever lose. He was without compare when the hot temper just beneath the surface erupted. Few who battled him lived to talk about it.

His stepmother looked up at the sky. "Do ye think we should set up camp as well?"

"Aye, it is best that we do. Horses can hurt themselves traveling in the dark."

Before long, they had a bonfire lit and a makeshift shelter for the women.

Fish were caught in a nearby stream and the meal was shared with the other travelers who seemed happy to have companions who would keep dangers at bay.

"Where exactly are ye headed?" Caelan asked one of the men, who'd introduced himself as Luke.

"To the shore. To find a village to settle at," he replied eyeing the bonfire. "I hope to find work and a home for my wife."

"My family owns the lands from here to the northern shore. There is a village there that is growing. It is called *Eilean Daes*. Ye may wish to settle there." Caelan admired the man, who seemed hopeful that he could provide his wife with a better life. He couldn't help but wonder what it would be like to begin again, without work, coin, or food.

"Reach out to my cousin. His name is Dougal Ross, and he is the village constable. He will help ye find shelter and work."

The man gave him a grateful look. "We are very fortunate to have met ye on the way to our new life."

Caelan did not ask the man why he and his companions were traveling. It was obvious they were poor and without resources. At the same time, Luke seemed proud and eager to find work. He had no doubt the man and his companions would do well in *Eilean Daes*.

Instead of sleeping, he took first watch and along with two guards patrolled while the others slept. Caelan wasn't keen to spend a night outdoors and then another day in the same clothes. Since very young unless at battle—which he dressed appropriately for—he changed clothes daily after washing up. They planned to remain with Stuart and Cait a fortnight, so he'd brought enough clothes to change daily with only needing a few things washed.

Thankfully since there was a creek not too far from where they camped, he could bathe and change at dawn. At the thought, he looked up to the star-filled sky. The moon was bright, giving plenty of light. Although the weather was quite cold, thankfully there were no clouds in the sky.

The last thing they needed was to travel through a storm.

AS SOON AS the first rays of daylight peeked, Caelan got up and grabbed clothes from the small trunk he'd packed.

He hurried to the creek, not looking forward to the frigid water, but the sooner he got it over with, the better. After looking to ensure the women were not up, he undressed and dove into the water. The coldness of it took his breath and he gasped before diving back in.

After running soap over his body, he submerged in the water and jumped back up, his teeth chattering as he waded to the shoreline.

When he turned to where he'd left his clothes, Glynis appeared through the trees. She yawned and stretched her arms over her head. Oblivious to his presence, she walked to the edge of the water and lowered to crouch near the water's edge.

Caelan was shivering and did not have the patience to wait for the woman to wash her face or whatever it was she was doing.

"Do ye mind turning yer back? I need to dress." Caelan knew he sounded irritated, but he didn't care.

When she turned to him, he dropped both hands to cover his sex. Sure, his lips were turning blue from the cold, he became more annoyed when instead of turning away, she stared at him, mouth agape.

"Why are bathing? The water is much too cold."

"If ye do not turn, I will not care what ye see," he snapped with little effect as the shivering made his voice quiver.

"Oh. Aye. Sorry." Glynis turned around and looked up at the trees. "Did ye sleep well?"

Struggling to put his tunic on, he grunted in response. Once it was on, the warmth of the thick fabric began to seep in making it easier to pull on his breeches.

He sat down to pull on his socks and boots and then tied a thick leather belt around his waist. Once that was done, he lifted his scabbard and sword.

"I need to wash my face and return to help my aunt," Glynnis said still standing in the same spot.

Without a response, Caelan walked away. The woman annoyed him. He'd taken an instant dislike to Glynis. Just her mere presence made him cross.

Perhaps he was set in his ways, preferring to spend time with those he knew. Yes, he enjoyed female company here and there, but only for short moments. This one, although pretty, rubbed him the wrong way with her way of speaking without thought.

At his home, most days after last meal, he and Beatrice, Duncan's wife, often spent time in the parlor reading or playing a game. She entertained him with her antidotes and many times they would laugh about the silliest things.

If he could meet someone like Beatrice, he might could see himself settling down. Though maybe not. Even though he enjoyed her company, it was nice when Beatrice went to seek her husband leaving Caelan to his own company and thoughts.

"Caelan?" His stepmother approached. "Have ye seen Glynis?"

He nodded. "She is by the creek."

"Alone?"

"She is not that far, just there." He pointed in the direction where he'd left Glynis.

His stepmother gave him a curious look. "Ye do not care for her. Why?"

He shrugged. "Just do not. No reason really."

"I am sure once we get to yer brother's, ye will not have to spend time with her daily." His stepmother frowned. "None-theless, she is under our care and it is yer responsibility to ensure her safety."

Escorting his stepmother to the creek, he searched the shoreline for Glynis. She was not where he'd left her. "She could be seeking privacy to relieve herself," he said when his stepmother became frantic.

"Glynis!" Lady Mariel called out. "Where are ye dear?"

There was a splash and Glynis popped out of the water just a few yards away. She hurried from the water and bare as a bairn rushed to her clothes. At hearing his stepmother call her name, Glynis stopped and turned to them giving him a view of her entire front side.

Caelan coughed to hide a bark of laughter.

"Ah!" She grabbed a skirt or something and held it up covering herself.

"Do not just stand there, ensure no one comes," his step-mother scolded.

The woman was truly an annoyance. He glared at his

stepmother who motioned for him to turn his back. Caelan turned and stood with feet apart and arms crossed while he assumed his stepmother helped Glynis dress quickly.

"What are ye thinking bathing in such cold water?" he called out.

There was no reply. He pressed his lips together at how Glynis had dashed from the water. Sputtering and stumbling to her clothing, her bare wet body glistening. She was exquisite if he were to be honest. Small waist, round hips, and large breasts. The type of body a man could become lost in.

"Caelan." His stepmother tapped his shoulder. "Let us get back to camp and see about getting on the road."

UPON REACHING THE outskirts of *Eilean Daes*, Stuart's lands, they separated from the travelers. Each group going their separate ways. Caelan reminded Luke to ask for his cousin, Dougal Ross, before their group headed down toward the seashore, as his party headed up the incline to where Stuart and his wife lived.

THE LANDS SURROUNDING Stuart and Cait's large stone house were beautiful. There were cattle and sheep grazing on the lush green hillside and they passed pens and corrals filled with more livestock as they neared the house.

Goats watched them with unblinking eyes and several chickens scurried out of the way, clucking in displeasure at their apparent rudeness.

STUART AND CAIT emerged from the house with expectant looks. Caelan dismounted and walked to his brother who hugged him tightly and pounded his back in greeting.

"Yer visit is most opportune," Stuart said. "It seems someone we did not ever wish to see again, has reared his head near here."

Caelan narrowed his eyes. "Cairn McInerny?"

"Aye."

His blood ran cold. "Then we must kill him."

CHAPTER TWO

GLYNIS IMMEDIATELY FELL in love with Cait Ross. The pretty woman was shy but had a strength about her that radiated.

Like Glynis and her mother back in Bara, Cait took part in every aspect of maintaining the large home. Just after they arrived, Cait along with two servant women, who she introduced as Maisie and Grace, served them a delicious meal. Cait's companion, Cora, helped as well.

After the meal, Cora poured hot cider and placed a tray of delicious tarts for the women to enjoy as they settled into chairs in front of a cheery fire. The front room of the house was spacious and spotless.

Glynis couldn't help but admire the simple but well-made furniture. She itched to explore the rest of the house and get ideas for when she too had her own home one day.

"Ye must drink the cider and ensure to keep warm," her aunt said in a chastising tone. She then looked to Cait. "She bathed in the creek this morning. The water had to be ice-cold."

Cait's eyes widened. "I cannot stand cold water. Ye should have waited and had a hot bath here."

"It was impulsive. I saw Caelan bathing and thought perhaps I should also..." Glynis stopped talking when she realized what she'd said. "I did not actually see him bathe… Oh, my." She covered her burning cheeks with both hands.

Cait and her aunt laughed.

"What exactly did ye see?" Cait asked her eyes bright with glee.

Her aunt gave her a pointed look. "Caelan definitely saw ye bare as a bairn getting out of the creek."

Her eyes rounded. "No."

"Aye," her aunt said. "So ye both had an interesting start to the day. Seeing each other naked."

When the women laughed, her cheeks hot with mortification Glynis had to join in. She'd not thought he'd seen her, but then again, she'd been in such a hurry to get out of the water it only made sense.

Just then Caelan walked in. At seeing him, both Cait and her aunt burst into loud laughter.

"What is so humorous?"

Her aunt smiled at him. "We are telling Cait and Cora about the bathing episodes this morning."

He narrowed his eyes at Glynis who pretended not to notice. "The cold does affect certain things."

After chuckling at his discomfort, his stepmother wiped tears from the corners of her eyes with a handkerchief. "It is quite funny; I am sorry that ye both are embarrassed."

"What exactly was affected?" Cait asked giving him an innocent look that did not fool anyone for an instant. Especially when the corners of her lips quivered.

"I came to inform ye, Stepmother," he began, ignoring Cait's question, "that I and the guards are going to ride about the area. We will be gone most of the day."

Cait looked to him again. “Is Stuart not going?”

“Only to the village, he has business to conduct.”

Glynis could not help but notice that he dressed differently here. He looked every inch a Scot. Wearing a thick woven tunic, leather boots, and wool breeches. In his hand, he held a fur-lined cloak that would keep him warm against the cold wind.

“Be with care,” Lady Mariel told him, her cheeks still pink from laughing.

Just before turning, he slid a glance toward her. Glynis wasn’t sure what to read in his gaze, but he certainly seemed to not care for her in the least.

When he’d gone out of earshot, she grimaced. “He does not like me.”

“Why would ye say that?” Cait asked. “He keeps stealing glances at ye.”

“Probably to ensure I keep a distance,” Glynis replied. “I said an impulsive thing at first meeting him and set the wrong tone.”

Lady Mariel lifted her cup and sipped. “Nonsense. Caelan is somewhat stern in his demeanor, but he doesn’t hold grudges. He is a fair man.”

Glynis wasn’t as sure. She stood and straightened her skirts. “If ye will excuse me, I need a bit of fresh air.”

Not waiting for a response, she went out the front door and headed to where Caelan and another man were saddling their horses.

“May I have a word?” Glynis said upon approaching.

Upon hearing her, Caelan looked surprised. “Aye, of course.” He held out the horse’s reins to the guard before walking toward her.

"Is something wrong?"

When Caelan met her gaze, she noted he had brilliant blue eyes that were heavily lashed. It wasn't the first time she'd noticed them, but now with the brightness of the day they seemed to stand out.

When his right brow lifted, she realized she must've been staring. "I-I . . . er. I wish to know why ye do not like me?"

"I have no reason to dislike ye, Glynis." His reply was flat, his expression blank. "Why would ye think it?"

His English accent made her pay extra attention to how he formulated words. If he were raised in England, it could be the reason for his rather cold demeanor. She'd often heard of how the English were aloof and rather reserved in their ways.

Now she'd gotten herself into another situation that would probably cause more awkwardness between them. "It seems, I cannot stop doing or saying things that annoy ye."

Caelan held out his right hand and she took it, unsure of what he planned. "Miss Glynis, I assure ye that I hold ye in the highest regard. Ye are important to my stepmother, whom I love dearly, and therefore ye must have some redeeming qualities."

He squeezed her hand and released it. "If ye will excuse me. I must go."

When he turned and walked away, she followed his progress unable to keep from studying his wide back, lean hips, and muscular legs.

Narrowing her eyes at his retreating back, she spoke out loud. "That was an insult."

If Caelan heard her, he didn't react. Instead, he mounted

and along with his guard escort rode from the courtyard. There wasn't a wall surrounding the area, so much as there were corrals and pens, so she could easily track them as they rode away until they disappeared past trees.

Just then her aunt appeared at the doorway and waved to her. "Come, we will help Cait make some blankets for when the bairn arrives."

IT WAS LATE by the time they put the finishing touches on the collection of small blankets they'd knitted. While Glynis sewed the edges, she peered out the window at the lowering sun.

"Are we to go to the village soon?"

Cait became animated. "Aye, we are. I wish to see Bree and am looking forward to introducing ye to her. We have become close friends since moving here and we visit often."

"Bree is the constable's wife," her aunt added. "She is married to my nephew, Dougal Ross."

"She is a lovely person, and ye will love the village. It is very pretty," Cait assured her.

Stuart Ross entered obviously returning from his trek to the village. Glynis studied him. With dark hair that flopped over his forehead giving him a roguish look, he was very attractive. He'd become more muscular over the years, and she wondered if Ewan had as well. She'd often had a hard time telling him and Ewan apart, they looked so much alike.

He smiled at her and went to kiss his mother on the temple. "I am so glad ye are here mother. Caelan was put out that ye had to spend the night outdoors."

Her aunt gave Stuart a bright smile. "Entirely my fault. There were some travelers that I stopped to speak to who were wary of traveling alone."

"Say no more," he replied with a chuckle. "These would be the people who arrived at the village earlier today and told of their good fortune to be escorted by Ross guards part of the way."

The man straightened and met Glynis' gaze. "It has been years since we saw each other."

"Aye," Glynis replied with a smile. "I was not sure at first if ye were Stuart or Ewan."

"They do look a great deal alike," Cait said pensively. "However, I believe Stuart is a bit taller."

He grinned. "And a better archer."

Her aunt laughed. "Let us prepare for last meal before he begins telling stories of how many times, he's beaten Ewan in competitions."

Everyone stood and walked to the adjoining dining room. Once there, Cait took her arm and guided her toward the kitchen. "Stuart, keep yer mother company."

"Ye must know that I am much too involved in the running of this household," Cait told her with a wide grin. "Much to the annoyance of Maisie and Grace, who run the kitchens and would prefer I left them to their tasks."

The women looked to their mistress with obvious endearment. "Aye, if we let her, she'd run us out," one of them said with mock annoyance.

Cait waved the woman's words away. "Today I am not going to interfere. I am going to show off our handiwork in the garden."

They walked outside and immediately Glynis was enthralled by the lush vegetation. "How do ye keep it so green?

The weather has been horribly cold and rainy."

"We surround it with thick fencing to keep the wind at bay and add straw around each plant to keep the roots warm. Thankfully, it has not frosted yet..." As Cait continued speaking, it occurred to Glynis that the woman was in love with not only her husband but her life.

Would she one day have the kind of life that would make her glow like the woman before her? Although she often daydreamed of her future, she could not picture exactly what she wanted. Now seeing the house and Cait's life, she could see it being the perfect life.

"Cait?" she interrupted. "How do ye think... I mean do ye expect everyone can find happiness like this?" Glynis motioned to the garden and the house. "Ye seem to have it all."

The woman sighed. "Aye. I do feel I have more than I could ever wish for. And now with the bairn on the way," she said, pausing to catch her emotions. "A few months ago, I almost lost Stuart. He was dying... So now we strive for happiness every day."

Glynis brushed her fingertips over the leaf of a nearby plant. "I do not aspire to much. However, I would love to be content with my life."

When Cait frowned and seemed about to ask her to elaborate, Glynis turned away. "It is quite chilly. Can we return inside?"

CHAPTER THREE

STUART PUSHED AWAY from the table in his small study and rubbed his eyes. "How can ye do this all the time? We have only just started and already my head is a jumbled mess."

"Ye need to pay attention. It is not so complicated." Caelan stood and stretched. "We've only began yesterday. In the next days, we will work on yer ledgers daily so that when I leave ye should be able to maintain them easily. Just a few hours a week."

"Hours?" Stuart groaned. "Or ye could come here every so often and do it for me."

"No."

His brother studied him. "Ye seem different. More sour than normal."

"Could be because ye are not trying to learn what I am teaching ye, instead yer acting like a spoiled lad," Caelan replied in a deep Scottish bur. "I am about done with ye."

It never failed, whenever he mocked his brother's accents, they loved it. Stuart grinned. "I do not like numbers and such."

"To the devil with ye then, Stuart," Caelan replied with an even deeper accent, much to Stuart's glee.

Caelan returned to his original accent. "Where do ye think Cairn has been hiding?"

Stuart shrugged. "I am not sure, but Artair heard he'd

ridden through the village. He tried to track him but lost the trail. Cairn must be up to something otherwise why return to Uist."

"We should advise Darach. He is the one Cairn would want to go after."

"Not if we hunt him down," Stuart replied, the ease of the past moments erased and replaced with a tight jawline.

Past the window, the guards who'd gone to scout the coastline, came into view. They were leading their horses toward the corrals. Caelan followed their progress. "Hopefully they will bring news."

"Ye are here to help me with the ledgers. Leave the hunt to Artair for now," Stuart reminded him.

Caelan shook his head. "That man tried to overthrow our family. Cairn McInerny does not deserve to live."

Cairn had been a close advisor to their father and someone they'd known since childhood. The betrayal was so much more than just the man's obsession with power. It was the fact that upon their father's death, he'd turned so many people against Darach and the family.

Just then Artair Ross entered. Their cousin was like a brother to them. He was their father's brother's son and had served as a guard at Ross Keep until recently.

The tall man filled the doorway, his hazel gaze taking them in for a moment. "I'd forgotten ye were here," he said in greeting to Caelan.

"Any news?" Stuart asked. "Did anyone spot the bastard?"

"Nay. He is quite clever. I do believe he travels with a group and they are keeping off the main roads."

Caelan considered for a moment and then spoke. "He has

to have been with Clan Uisdein since disappearing. I am sure they gave him harbor."

"Why return?" Stuart asked. "There is nothing here in Uist for him except certain death if we catch him."

"Exactly," Caelan replied. "What about his family? They live near the village close to my home. Perhaps he travels there to see to a family matter."

"I will go there," Artair said, but stopped when Caelan shook his head. "We need to wait. If I am right, he is going there because someone has sent for him. If someone else has plans against us, we must find out who. We must send a spy that no one will suspect."

"Anton," Stuart stated. "My squire is up for a task such as this. He has family there he can visit. I trust him to not act suspiciously. He is very astute."

Artair left to find the squire, while Caelan insisted they return to the ledgers for a while longer.

"What do ye think of the lass, Glynis?" Stuart asked a short while later, as Caelan looked over his entries.

Caelan shrugged. "She is bothersome."

"It could be she was sent by the MacNeil in hopes of finding her a husband."

"I am not a true Ross, so a match with me would be of no real advantage."

His brother stood and rounded the table so fast, Caelan prepared to be hit. "Do not ever say that again. Ye are a Ross. Father ensured ye had the surname."

"I am bastard born, and everyone knows it. With or without the name."

"And a true member of our clan and family. Why would ye

say ye are not a true Ross?" His brother's expression left no room for argument.

Blowing out a breath Caelan had to smile. "Put yer chemise back on Stuart, I am not stating I do not feel like part of the family. I am stating how other lairds would see me."

At his statement, Stuart huffed. "Ye are my brother and I do not wish for ye to ever think we consider ye less than ourselves."

"I have absolutely no doubts about ye or any of our brother's feelings. I am fortunate to have such staunch alliance from all of ye."

In truth, Caelan often forgot he was half-sibling to the five men whom he'd come to love dearly. He had two sets of half brothers, the Ross brothers and his mother's other two sons. However, it was with the Ross clan that he found himself at home and more accepted.

He was friendly with his other brothers, but they were more reserved with their affection as they'd not grown up together.

The Ross brothers were fiercely loyal to one another and that included him. In return, he was the same way and would not hesitate to give his life to defend any of them.

"I think ye should consider courting Glynis," Stuart said pouring whiskey into a glass. "She is bonnie and has no husband."

Caelan eyed the drink in Stuart's hand. "Put the drink down. I know what ye are trying to do. To distract me. Ye cannot drink and work on ledgers."

"What about…" Stuart began, but Caelan cut him off.

"The more ye try to distract me, the longer we will remain

in here."

When Stuart returned to sit across from him, Caelan slid a look past him to the doorway. Glynis was a beauty; however, he was not interested in courting or God forbid marrying any time soon.

THE DINING ROOM was full for last meal. Dougal Ross and his wife Bree came for a visit adding to the merriment.

His stepmother and Glynis were joined by Bree, Cait, Ana, and Clara, Cait's mother, at a table along with another woman he understood to be the wife to one of the men who worked there. He was used to the animated discussions of the women back at Keep Ross. However, since this house was much smaller, their voices filled the room giving the meal a cheerful feel.

Caelan sat with Stuart, Artair, Dougal, and their uncle, Lyall Ross, who'd come to live with Stuart and Cait. They were joined by a pair of guards who'd been traveling with Artair.

"I may join you in learning to keep ledgers. I need to learn about keeping track of expenses and such," Dougal said. "I have more things to keep an eye on now that I live in the village. There is livestock and other items that I am accountable for."

"Ye will not like it," Stuart said. "I do not know why it must be so complicated."

"Because ye have to ensure not to be giving or spending more than ye have. It is important to know where all yer holdings are and how much ye maintain," Caelan explained with much more patience than he felt.

The truth was his mind was on Cairn and what the man

had done. If it were up to him, he would have left the morning after arriving and gone to find him.

There was nothing lower than a traitor and a coward, in Caelan's opinion. A man who betrayed those who'd fed and clothed him for years did not deserve to live.

As soon as the meal ended and the men moved to the front room to relax and drink, he slipped out the back door and went around the house to the guard homes. There were three small houses, two belonged to the guards and the third was where Artair lived. He knocked on the first door and it was opened by a young man who grinned at him.

"Mister Caelan," Anton said. "What can I do for ye?"

"I wish to speak to ye in private." He motioned for the young man to follow. "About the matter I am sure Artair has spoken to ye about. It will require yer prompt attention."

Caelan went on to explain to Anton about Cairn. "As ye are aware, it is imperative ye are not caught. If Cairn happens to see ye, pretend not to remember who he is. He is as wily as he is dangerous."

"I do not believe it will be a challenge, as I have never had an exchange with him. He usually ignored the servants."

This was good. "Ye never had a conversation with him?"

"Nay," Anton said shaking his head. "I do not recall ever even being in the same room with him. Other than perhaps in the courtyard at some point. I am fairly certain he would never recognize me."

"Good."

"When should I leave?"

"Tomorrow morning. Ye should be there by evening. Bide yer time, go about yer day as usual when visiting. But keep a keen eye out."

Anton nodded. "And ears as well."

Walking back to the house, Caelan felt good. Anton was bright and would in all probability be able to gather much more information than he or his brothers could. All that remained was to hope that Cairn stayed in the village long enough for Anton to discover what he was planning and where he would go next.

He hesitated at a window. Inside the room Glynis stalked to and fro, seeming to be upset about something. She held her hands up to her chest and had her head bent. It was a moment before he realized she was not upset but was instead praying. He would not have taken her for a pious woman. If anything, after the episode at the creek, he thought her more spirited than spiritual.

She did have a delightful body. Even now he could clearly picture her full breasts and round bottom. And he found the shape of her legs very enticing. He would not mind delving into her and running his hands and mouth over every inch of her body.

"There ye are." His stepmother walked toward him, and he looked up to the sky, pretending to be engrossed in the passing clouds.

She looked to the window. "I wondered where she'd gone off to." Her lips curved. "Ye seemed enthralled by her.

"I was actually deep in thought Stepmother," Caelan replied in a crisp tone. "I would not have taken Glynis for a pious woman. Yet she seems to be praying fervently."

"It is understandable," his stepmother replied looking toward the window. "She finds herself in quite a predicament."

"What kind of..."

"Forget I said anything," she interrupted. "I came to ask ye about Stuart and the ledgers. He seems to find it rather daunting."

"It is not beyond his grasp. However, for someone who prefers the outdoors, archery, and battle training, doing the opposite is hard."

He truly wished to help his brother. Stuart was not at all interested in bookkeeping and it would become problematic if he let it fall by the wayside.

"I could remain longer and ensure everything is set up. Then return regularly to help. Make it easier for him to keep up."

She walked beside him and slipped her arm through his. "Cait might could do it. She is a fast learner and took quickly to reading and writing. Isobel even began to teach her some numbers."

They continued to discuss alternatives to Stuart being forced into doing something he so detested until they arrived back at the house, Caelan hesitated. "Stepmother, do not try to do any matchmaking between myself and Glynis. I am not interested."

"I doubt the lass is interested in courtship. She came to South Uist for a reason."

Again she did not elaborate, which despite himself, piqued his interest.

"Stepmother, why is she here?" Caelan took her elbow. "Ye act as if something horrible has happened to her."

His stepmother gave him a soft smile. "Nothing so horrible that time away will not help. I assure ye, it is nothing to worry yerself over. I can only tell ye that she is here to heal."

With that, his stepmother walked away.

A scant second later, Glynis rushed past him. Her face was bright as she looked to him. "I am to learn to ride a horse today."

He followed her. "Who is going to teach ye?"

"The guard called... Ian, I believe. He overheard me telling my aunt how much I wished to learn so that I can ride places without waiting for someone to take me."

When he continued to walk alongside, she gave him a questioning look. "Why are ye following me?"

"Why have ye not learned to ride before?"

She faltered and stopped walking. "No reason. Please go see about yer lessons with Stuart. I must find Ian."

"Does Stepmother know what ye are about?"

"Aye, I just walked past her in the kitchen." She motioned to the doorway. "Will ye go away?"

"No," Caelan wasn't sure why, but he was sure the reason Glynis wished to learn to ride had something to do with what his stepmother had alluded to. "I will teach ye to ride, but not today. It is about to rain."

Glynis looked up and indeed clouds were gathering. She frowned at the sky. "Most bothersome. I have only a fortnight to learn. I cannot wait. I do not mind getting wet."

Just as she was about to turn away, he took her by the arm. "Ye are the most headstrong person I have ever met. I said no."

It took several seconds for Caelan to realize that the pain radiating up his body was due to the hard hit between his legs from her knee. He fell sideways to the ground, letting out a loud groan when his head hit a rock.

"Oh, dear," Glynis stood over him, her eyes wide. "What have I done?"

Caelan tried to reply, but all he could manage was a croak. Lucky, since he'd tried to utter a vile curse.

She tugged at his arm. "Get up before my aunt sees. I do not wish to upset her."

"Let me go," Caelan managed finally able to speak. Tentatively releasing his hold from between his legs, he blew out a long breath. Doing his best to ignore the hovering woman, he got to his feet, bending at the waist as he stood.

"If ye do not go into the house, I will not be held responsible for what I do next." His tone left absolutely no room for argument. When he straightened and glared down at her, Glynis' eyes rounded, and she turned on her heel and dashed into the house.

"Vile wench," he muttered and walked slowly over to lean on a fence.

"Want to ride to the village with me?" Artair walked from the direction of the stables. "Was that Glynis I saw racing to the house?"

Caelan nodded. "She planned to take riding lessons. I said no and she is angry."

His cousin laughed. "A feisty lass then?"

"An annoying one. I prefer to keep my distance from her. However, I am responsible for her safety and will not have her breaking her neck while under my authority."

At hearing his voice, his horse neared and nudged his arm. He produced a carrot and fed it to the delighted animal.

"I will go with ye. First, let me speak to Stepmother I do

not wish for Glynis to take advantage of my absence and defy me."

Artair walked alongside as they went toward the house. Obviously, he expected some sort of entertainment if the women turned against Caelan.

Inside the front room, his stepmother and Cait sat working on whatever item they made. Both looked up and his stepmother frowned at him.

"What did ye do to Glynis? She looked quite upset when she walked in."

"I told her she could not take riding lessons from one of the guards. I will not have her injured while under my authority. And she kicked me."

The women exchanged surprised looks.

His stepmother neared. "She struck ye?"

"Aye, but it is of no consequence unless I desire to produce heirs to my bastardom."

Artair choked while trying to keep from laughing, his stepmother on the other hand looked directly to the injured area. "Perhaps a cold compress. Go to the bedchamber and remove yer bottoms."

At this, his cousin burst into laughter.

"I will be fine. Artair and I are going to the village. Please do not allow Glynis out of yer sight. Her temperament will be sensed by the horse and she will no doubt be stomped to death."

Cait pressed her lips together and her brows lowered. He wasn't sure if she was embarrassed or trying to keep from laughing. His stepmother on the other hand huffed. "Caelan, I am sure she is mortified by her actions. I will speak to her and ensure she makes amends."

"Tell her to stay away from me. That will be enough."

"ARE YE COMFORTABLE?" Artair asked. There was no humor in his tone.

Caelan set his back teeth at the reminder. "Not as comfortable a ride as I would have wanted."

"What would bring her to act so violently?" Artair asked. "It could be her bright red hair."

For a moment he considered what his stepmother alluded to—her healing. "Or she's had to protect herself from an attack recently."

The seashore came into view and they brought their horses to a stop. The picturesque village with a smattering of recently rebuilt cottages and shops was inviting. Fishing boats bobbed out in the blue-gray water, and in the distance a pair of bìrlinns made their way through the choppy waters.

"Where do ye suppose those bìrlinns come from?" Caelan said following their progress.

Artair frowned. "Benbecula or North Uist. I am not sure. Hopefully not the Uisdein's out to cause more trouble."

They rode in the direction of their cousin Dougal's house. Hopefully he would know if visitors were expected.

Just before they arrived, they saw a party of guards, that included Stuart, riding toward Dougal's house as well.

Upon spotting them, Stuart rode over to them.

Caelan pointed out to the sea. "Expecting visitors?"

For a long moment, Stuart tracked the bìrlinns. "Often people come to trade with the people in the village. Usually, the visitors are friendly. We can only watch and see."

Stuart motioned for one of the guards to come near. "Go and ask Dougal about any expected visitors. Inform him of the two bìrlinns approaching."

The guard rode off while Caelan and his cousins remained atop the hill watching as the bìrlinns maneuvered away from the village to another shoreline.

"That doesn't bode well," Stuart said grimly. "Why are they going to where there are no people?"

"Is there another village north of here?" Caelan asked.

"Aye, there is. They are not Clan Ross, but a distant relative of the Macdonald. Not a friendly bunch."

The guard returned with a message from Dougal to come for a meal.

"Obviously he is not worried," Artair said as they guided their mounts in the direction of the Dougal's house that sat atop a hill.

Caelan looked back toward the sea. "Or he does not wish to impart the information through a guard."

As they entered the house, they were greeted by the aroma of baking meat pies. The delicious smell had them hurrying to remove their cloaks and scabbards and get into the dining room.

As soon as they sat, a young maid placed cups of ale before them, and Bree brought a platter piled high with meat pies. "I was just telling Dougal that I'd made much too many. But it seems there was a reason for it," she told them with a bright smile.

Caelan had met Bree only a few times. The woman was friendly and warm, always seeming to be in a cheerful mood. Quite the opposite of the hateful Glynis. "Bree, do ye plan to spend time with Glynis?" He wasn't sure why he asked.

"Aye. She, Cait, and yer stepmother are coming to spend a couple of days here the day after tomorrow." She gave him a questioning look. "Why do ye ask?"

He looked up at her with lifted brows. "Perhaps some of yer pleasant personality can help hers."

Bree laughed and shook her head. "I am sure it is not as bad as ye think."

"Somewhat," Artair said. "She is quite fiery."

Dougal hurried into the room. "I apologize for not greeting ye. I sent a man to see about those bìrlinns and find out who they are here to visit with."

"I was going to ask that we do that," Stuart said. "Ye know something?"

Shaking his head, Dougal took a long sip of ale and waited for his wife to leave the room. "I do not expect it is good. It is the second set of bìrlinns in a sennight. Each of them with at least twenty men. The last two landed just north of here."

Stuart shook his head. "If they were going to the Macdonald village, they would not go by here. I suppose we can go there and speak to whoever is laird over them. I do not think they have close ties with the Macdonalds our brothers are married to."

"That is another thing we need to find out. Perhaps send a guard to inform Darach and to ask Isobel about any relationship with them," Caelan said.

The many questions hung in the air as they ate the flavorful meat pies. Despite the niggling feeling what happened could be tied to the sudden appearance of Cairn, Caelan could not decide if he should bring it up.

"Hopefully Anton will find out if Cairn is indeed in the southern village as soon as he arrives," Stuart commented.

There was understanding in Stuart's gaze. They were both thinking along the same lines. If Cairn recruited cutthroats to try anything against their clan, they were about to go to war again.

CHAPTER FOUR

GLYNIS SAT UP from the bed. Her eyes were dry and swollen from crying. Over and over, she relived what she'd done. The Ross' were hosting her, helping her get away from a bad situation and she'd repaid them by acting like a child.

It was certain her aunt would send her back and she wasn't ready to return home. The guilt that assaulted her each time she saw her brother, added to the blame she was sure her parents laid at her feet for what she had done, kept her stomach in knots.

After a rap on the door, her aunt entered with a cup in her hand. "I boiled a few herbs to help calm ye."

Glynis stood and rushed to her aunt. She hugged her tightly. "I am so very sorry. Please forgive me."

"Dear, ye are making me spill the tea," her aunt said quietly.

When Glynis released her, Lady Mariel placed the cup on a table and motioned to a pair of chairs. The bedchamber was tiny, both she and Caelan were staying in servant's rooms as there was limited space in the house. There were four servant rooms on one side of the house, two of which were left empty for guests. And the three rooms on the opposite side of the house were for Cait and Stuart, and the third was currently shared by her aunt and Cait's mother.

"I understand ye have gone through a hard time," her aunt began. "However, ye must do yer best to control yer emotions. Ye are not reckless by nature. A bit feisty, aye, I grant ye, but to have injured my son that is not acceptable."

Heat surged up from her neck, and she was sure her face burned a bright red. "I do not know what came over me. I just keep seeing them."

Her already tender eyes stung with unshed tears. "My recklessness is what gave those men the opportunity for the attack. I cannot stop thinking about the horrible sight when they attacked Gavin and left him for dead. All because of me."

"It was not yer fault. Those men's actions were their own choice."

"If I had not gone out alone. It would not have happened. It is absolutely my fault."

"And now ye are rude to men in an effort not to give them thoughts that could lead to it happening again?"

Glynis hung her head with no idea why she did anything as of late. It was as if her body and mind were not connected and her actions instinctive. Caelan had not meant any harm; however, her reaction had been so violent. Not called for in the least.

"What is happening to me?" Glynis covered her face as tears slid down her cheeks. "I am damaged, Aunt Mariel. I do not think to ever recover from this."

"Ye will, but ye must be patient."

She worried about facing Caelan when he returned from the village. One word from him and she could be sent back. There would be no questioning his response to what she'd done.

"Would ye like to make bread pudding?" her aunt asked, catching her off guard.

"Pudding?" she repeated, unsure why her aunt would plan to cook at a time like this. "Aye, of course. It is my favorite."

Her aunt pushed the cup into her hands. "Very well. Drink this. Wash yer face. And meet me in the kitchen."

ADMITTEDLY, WHILE TEARING the stale bread into chunks and then stirring together the milk, eggs, honey, and spices, Glynis was able to take her mind from her troubles.

"Pour the egg mixture over the crumbs," her aunt directed as she chopped figs and a pair of peeled apples.

Once they mixed everything together, they wrapped the mixture in a cloth to steam it. Whilst the pudding steamed, they drank hot cider just outside the door. The combination of the heat of the kitchen at their backs and the feeble sunlight on their legs made for a perfect repose.

"I wish I could have a home such as this," Glynis said wistfully. "I may ask Father to build a cottage where I can live alone and spend my days gardening, cooking, and sewing. I do not require anything else."

Her aunt let out a sigh. "I must admit to finding life here away from all the comings and goings of the keep, rather relaxing. However, after a fortnight, I am more than ready to return to my life there."

"I do not know what to do?" Glynis admitted. "I do not wish to return home. My brother, although recovered, will never be the same. His face is disfigured forever. Each time I see him, I want to cry."

"Were the men caught?"

Glynis shrugged. "The one my brother injured was. The other two are still about somewhere. When I ask about it, I am told not to fret."

"Oh, dear. I am sure they will be caught eventually." Her aunt patted her hand. "But ye must decide what to do with yer life, Glynis. Ye cannot hide from things. I understand how ye must feel—"

"If ye wish me to return home I will. I do not want to be a burden. Especially given what I did." Tears spilled down her cheeks and Glynis sniffed loudly. Thankfully, Maisie and Grace had invited Clara to visit their family and would be gone for a few days, so her distress didn't have more witnesses.

Her aunt gave her a stern look. "Stop yer crying Dear. I do not think ye are ready to return home."

Glynis nodded. "I will try. I promise."

"Good lass." After a hesitation, she added, "Speak with Caelan. He is very patient and as I've told ye, he does not hold grudges. Not with family." Her aunt smiled and it was obvious she was very fond of Caelan.

Her aunt continued. "As a young man, he was teased mercilessly because of his accent and being so different. Every time it happened, he would seek me out and we would speak about it. Most of the time he defended those who treated him badly, understanding that they found him different."

"He allowed it to continue?" Glynis was surprised that he would be so forgiving.

Her aunt chuckled. "He never got the chance to do much

about it. My other sons ensured anyone who mistreated Caelan was taught a lesson. Oftentimes, sending the offender off with a limp or blackened eye."

"It is nice to have family defend ye," Glynis said with a sigh. "My brothers are the same."

"Ye would do the same for them would ye not? Ye'd rather suffer an injury than allow one of them to be hurt."

Glynis had not considered that her brother felt that way. He'd often repeated to her that given the choice, he'd do the same again.

"Aye, I would, a thousand times over."

They remained sipping their cider in silence, the aroma of the steamed pudding wafting around them.

"It smells delightful." Cait walked into the kitchen looking well rested from her nap. "We should start last meal. Although, I am at a loss as to what to cook today."

"A simple chicken stew will do," Aunt Mariel replied. "I've already asked one of the lads to see about killing two chickens and plucking them clean. All we must do is find some potatoes and carrots. There are already onions in the baskets there." She pointed to a gardening basket on one of the shelves.

"I will make bread," Glynis offered and stood up.

Cait hugged her, the action sending warm tendrils of caring through her. "I am so glad ye came here, Glynis. Ye will find happiness, I just know it."

"Do not make her cry again," her aunt said with a huff. "Go on now, each of ye to yer tasks."

IT WAS MUCH later when the deep voices of the men sounded in the front room. Glynis' stomach tumbled. She had to face Caelan and apologize.

Her aunt didn't seem to notice that she hesitated at putting bread into a platter to be served. Loaf held in her hand as she listened to the voices.

Moments later, Stuart rushed into the kitchen and wrapped Cait in a hug from behind as she placed bowls onto a tray. Cait smiled up at her husband who kissed her temple.

"Whatever it is yer cooking smells delicious," Stuart said grinning at her and his mother. "We are quite hungry."

"I am sure Bree fed ye well. Ye have just turned into gluttons," her aunt teased.

"True," Artair said entering the kitchen. "We restrained and did not eat any of the meat pies she sent to ye." He lifted a basket. "There are six in here."

"Six?" Her aunt took the basket. "That means ye each ate one."

Artair frowned. "Why would ye think that?"

Her aunt rolled her eyes. "Because Bree would have sent one for Masie, Grace, and Carla, as well. She did not know they'd not be here."

Stuart laughed. "Mother ye are very intelligent."

"Which means, the lot of ye are not that hungry."

Caelan entered and stood at the door with his arms crossed and a warm expression on his face. His lips curved at the interchange between his stepmother and the others. "I did not eat one. Artair ate two."

When his stepmother glared at Artair, Caelan laughed.

Artair glowered. "Ye did not have to tell."

Caelan looked at her as she tried her best to blend into the background. Glynis was sure to present a horrible sight. Swollen eyes, flour on her face, and disheveled hair.

Caelan studied her for a moment, his gaze moving from her face to the bread tray. Then to her utter shock, his lips curved. Not into a wide smile, but just enough that she let out a breath, her gaze locking with his.

After the meal ended, she insisted she be allowed to clean up alone. Her aunt looked tired and Cait was preoccupied with her husband. Artair had gone to his house and she assumed Caelan was either in the front room or in his bedchamber.

She emptied the leftovers into a bucket and carried it out to the pigpen. She'd noted that was what Maisie did after every meal. Having added stale bread to the bucket there was plenty, and she was glad because two rather rotund pigs greeted her with loud happy grunts as she emptied the contents into their trough.

She went to the well and got water to rinse out the bucket so it would not stink in the kitchen. Then she refilled it with clean water to use to finish the cleaning.

In the kitchen she scrubbed the trays and table, then wrapped the leftover bread pudding in a thick cloth so they could slice it and reheat it in the morning.

"Ye are quite adept at chores." A deep voice made her jump and turn to see who it was. Although she recognized it to be Caelan, she had to be sure.

"Everyone helps out in my home. We all cook, clean, and take care of the livestock. It is a good thing I think." Glynis spoke without looking at him directly.

"It is good." He walked around the table and lifted a kettle.

"What are ye doing? I can do it for ye." She watched as he walked around the kitchen, seeming at ease in the space.

"I like to drink tea in the evening and usually make it myself."

"Tea?" Glynis frowned. "Is that boiled herbs?"

"Dried herbs, yes. Tea leaves." He produced a pouch and held it out to her.

Not sure what to do, she took it and sniffed it. It was a rather pleasant smell, which made her curious to know how it tasted.

"I will make enough so ye can taste it," Caelan said. He filled the kettle with water, placed it on a hook and then put it over the fire.

While the water heated, he found two cups and then walked out. Moments later, he returned with milk.

"I must apologize profusely," Glynis finally said watching him place the dried herbs into a smaller linen pouch. "I cannot forgive myself for what I did. Can ye ever forgive me?"

His blue gaze met hers for a short instant. "I do not know what ye went through, but it does not excuse what ye did."

He'd not accepted her apology. His tone although not cold, was not warm either. It was as if he spoke about nothing more than the weather.

"How do ye feel?" Glynis asked.

"Riding all day has kept ye on the forefront of my mind."

"Oh." Glynis wasn't sure what she could do. "My aunt suggested a cold compress..." she hesitated. "I can get some cloths and a bowl of water. I am sure it will be soothing."

After seeping the tea bags and adding milk, he handed her a cup and then stood with the other cup in his hand. "I will take ye up on the cold compress. I will await ye in my bedchamber." With that he walked out.

Glynis had not meant to do it for him, but to provide the items. She bit her bottom lip. "I do owe it to him to ensure he does not suffer."

Letting out a breath, she tasted the tea and found it very delicious. Once she brought Caelan the water and cloths, she would sit and drink it.

This was certainly a very trying day.

CHAPTER FIVE

IT WAS CRUEL of him to ask Glynis to see about his injury. He had planned to apply cold compresses before going to sleep in hopes of not waking up sore. Glynis had kneed him hard, and his bruised sack remained tender. The horseback riding had not helped in the least.

It was good that she offered to bring the water and cloths. That way he could remove his britches and sit in only his long tunic while enjoying his tea and allowing the sore area a reprieve from constriction.

Moments later there was a soft knock and she pushed the already half ajar door open further. She peered in, her gaze automatically going to his bare legs.

"The water is very chilled," she said softly placing a bowl on the small table next to him. Then she produced two folded cloths. "See that ye do not get the floor too wet."

With that, she looked to his legs again then turned and hurried to the door.

Caelan stood. "Glynis."

She froze and turned slowly. "Aye?"

He stood and closed the distance between them. Caelan peered down at her. So close to her, he had to fight the urge to touch her. The soft edge of her jawline that led to a rather desirable long neck was made for lingering kisses.

"It is kind of ye to bring me the water."

Her eyes rounded at his nearness. A slow pink color traveled from her neck up to her cheeks, and when her lips parted, he could not look away.

"It is the least I could do," she replied, surprising him. "My actions were uncalled for and ye are still in pain."

He couldn't help the smile that curved his lips. "Aye, I am."

"I am so very sorry." She started to turn away, but he took her arm. This time gently.

"Why do ye fight so hard?"

"I do not fight," Glynis looked to where his hand wrapped around her upper arm. "I should go." Lifting her chin, she gave him a challenging look.

Later he would realize that he'd done all in his power to keep her from leaving his room. However in that moment, without knowing why, he pressed a soft kiss to her lips then released her arm.

With a sharp intake of breath, Glynis' gaze bore into his and then to his shock, she rolled her eyes, turned, and walked out.

Caelan couldn't help but chuckle at her reaction. It was the first time a lass acted as if he had absolutely no idea how to kiss. To his annoyance, it felt like a challenge. To convince Glynis that he could kiss her senseless. He wanted very much to kiss her again and this time elicit a very different reaction.

NO SOONER DID Caelan wake, than there was a knock on his

door. He opened it to find the guard who'd gone to speak to Darach.

"What is it?" he asked wondering why the man came to him.

"Artair said to come speak to ye. He was mounted and heading to the village when I arrived a few moments ago."

The young guard had been in the family's service since a lad and now was one of their best scouts. "The laird said to tell ye he will be sending one hundred men and they will arrive by tonight. Once that happens, he wishes for ye to go see about the encroachers and warn them off."

For the most part, Caelan was rarely part of any battle plan. He remained on the fringes of such things, unless specifically ordered to do something different by his brother. The only time he'd not had to be asked was when one of his brother's life was threatened. Otherwise, he stayed behind to stand in for Darach.

This time he understood why he was ordered to go. Stuart had a wife and a bairn on the way, so Darach preferred that he remain in his role of archer, in the safety of the archer ranks behind the warriors.

On the other hand, because he was an accomplished swordsman, Caelan would be the one negotiating and approaching the men who were gathering on the shore.

"Go and seek yer rest. I will see about speaking to my brother and ensuring all will be ready when the warriors arrive."

Upon entering the dining hall, the only people awake were Glynis and his stepmother. They were in the kitchen talking softly while drinking something in cups. He suspected his stepmother had found his stash of tea.

"Stepmother," he said in greeting and then looked at Glynis, "Glynis."

His stepmother waved him closer. "Ye must procure more of this for me. I find it a perfect thing to drink in the morning."

"I brought ye a parcel of it last year. It must still be in the kitchen at the keep." Caelan went past them to the tea kettle. "When do the cooks return?"

"Tomorrow," Glynis replied. "Is there something ye require that is not provided for ye?" Her tone was flat. Disinterested.

Caelan couldn't help but give her a challenging look. "Darach is sending one hundred men. They arrive tomorrow, probably late in the day."

"Ah," his stepmother said, not seeming to be bothered by the news of a hundred more mouths to feed. "I will ask the young lads to see about butchering a pig."

Just then Stuart walked in, his gaze moving from Glynis and his mother's cups to the fire.

"There is a porridge boiling and we will toast leftover bread pudding," their mother said by way of greeting.

Glynis stood and began the task of slicing the bread pudding and within moments, bowls of porridge and toasted pudding were prepared for them along with cups of cider.

"She is proficient," Stuart said, seeming surprised. "Strange."

"Glynis informed me yesterday that she and her mother share in the household duties in her home," Caelan told his brother as they walked out of the kitchen.

Moments later, Artair, Cait, Glynis, and his stepmother joined them in the dining room to enjoy first meal.

"Why are the men coming?" his stepmother asked.

Stuart gave him a look to ensure he softened his reply.

"This territory has been neglected for too long. The men must familiarize themselves with every part of Ross lands."

"Are ye going with them?" Cait asked, her gaze pinning Stuart with a look stating she knew they were leaving something out.

"Aye," Stuart replied. "These are my lands and I too need to ensure I know every part. It is necessary in order to keep our family as safe as possible."

"What about the ledgers?" Cait continued. "Ye and Caelan have barely spent any time."

"I will spend several more days tutoring my thickheaded brother before I leave, I assure ye," Caelan told her. "And I am not so far away that I cannot return occasionally to help."

Stuart looked to Artair. "Ye do not have to go."

Understanding that his cousin was charging him with protecting the house, Artair nodded. "Aye, I have much to do here."

Caelan finished his meal and stood. "Brother, let us spend today with yer ledgers." He almost chuckled when Stuart could not refuse and reluctantly stood.

They went to a small study that was tucked to the right of the main room, with only a table and four chairs. There was a small window that allowed enough light in to brighten the room. Other than that, there was little else in the room besides the ledgers, ink wells, and quills.

"A proper study should have a sideboard to pace in front

of," Caelan told his brother as he settled into a chair opposite him. "How else do ye plan to make sense of the numbers?"

Stuart frowned and changed the subject. "I wonder if it is possible that Cairn is the one gathering men on the shore."

"I do not think so. However, we will not know for sure until we go there."

His brother nodded. "I could not sleep last night contemplating what he is up to."

It was obvious that neither of them would be able to concentrate on the ledgers that day.

The statement echoed his own thoughts and Caelan nodded. "I have considered that perhaps him being sighted traveling south was a ruse. Meant to lull us into thinking he was heading to visit his family."

"That way he hoped the men could gather on the shoreline without us taking notice." Stuart let out a breath. "Should we split up and come at them from two sides?"

Caelan was not as well versed in battle as his brothers. The best ones to plan such things were Stuart and Darach.

"Four bìrlinns were spotted, each with about twenty men. That means there are at least eighty to our one hundred. If that is so, then we do not have much to worry about."

They considered what was the best course of action until Artair entered. The warrior limped a bit. He'd tried to hide it, but Caelan had noticed it the day before.

"What happened to yer leg?" Stuart asked.

At first, it was obvious Artair was going to deny any injury. Finally, he lowered to a chair and admitted what had happened. "I got kicked by a horse several days ago. It continues to bother me."

Stuart glared at their cousin. "Ye should not have been out

riding."

"I am fine," Artair snapped back. "The leg will repair on its own."

"Ye would not be able to walk on a broken leg, but ye should be with care." Caelan studied Artair, fear settling in his stomach. If it was so severe that the man lied, then it had to be bad.

"Show me," Stuart said standing. "Now."

Caelan prepared to break them up as Artair looked about to explode with fury. After a moment, he blew air out of his nose and pressed his lips together. "A horse did kick me. But it was weeks ago." He rubbed his right thigh. "My leg has not been the same since. I can barely sleep at night lately."

"Mother will help," Stuart said.

Artair nodded. "I will speak to her about it."

Mollified, Stuart let out a breath. "Caelan and I were discussing the best approach for the warriors the day after tomorrow."

"Split up. Come from both sides and some in the center. We should send in a smaller party first and upon them taking notice the rest rush in."

It sounded like a good plan to Caelan, except for one thing. "Can we, do it? We do not know the land."

"There is that," Stuart said. "There are a lot of inlets that may make it impossible for us to come from the north."

"Even from the south," Artair said. "I will get with the scouts that have gone out and with their help draw up a good map." The warrior groaned when he stood, no longer hiding his injury. "And I will speak to Aunt Mariel about my leg."

Left alone, Caelan motioned to the ledger atop the table. "Let us spend a few hours working."

CHAPTER SIX

DESPITE THE BUSYNESS of having to prepare for the men who'd be arriving the next day, Glynis found herself constantly recalling the night before. Why had Caelan kissed her? It was a soft kiss, more like a friendly sort. Though it felt as if it was more than that. Was he testing her to see how far he could take things?

Of course, she would never allow for anything to happen between them. Up until that moment, she was convinced he did not care for her in the least. As a matter of fact, she still felt that way. The only reason he'd kissed her was because of that. To catch her off guard for what reason, she wasn't sure.

"Is yer head in the clouds, Glynis?" Cait teased. When Glynis started and looked to her, she smiled. "I am asking if ye would consider remaining here after Lady Mariel and Caelan leave?"

"Oh," she replied her eyes widening. "It is lovely here. I would love to. What a kind offer."

Her aunt studied her. "What has ye so bothered now dear?"

"I apologized to Caelan for what I did yesterday." She blinked as tears threatened once again. "He did not accept it."

"Ye should not worry about it," Cait said. "I am sure he is not cross with ye. He seemed in good spirits this morning."

"But why did he not say he accepted my apology and that we should forget it," Glynis insisted. "It is bothering me. I do not know him like ye do."

Her aunt shook her head. "Ye are worrying yerself over nothing. I doubt he is thinking about it at all. He may have accepted but given his formality ye misunderstood."

Glynis was struck silent. Was that what the kiss meant? Goodness. She knew very little about the English. Was that how they accepted apologies?

ARTAIR SAT BACK, his injured leg lifted up onto another chair as Grace wrapped it with cloths that had been soaked in herbs. If he were to be honest, he doubted the herbs helped at all. The wrapping however did soothe the pains.

His aunt hovered over him; her brow pinched. "It is badly bruised Artair. Ye should have said something immediately upon the horse kicking ye."

"I expected for it to get better. But instead, it became more and more painful."

Grace, being an older woman, patted his foot in a motherly gesture. "Keep yer leg still. No moving about. We will bring yer meals here."

They left and he kept watch out the window. Tomorrow the men would arrive and go see about the encroachers. He hated to miss out on it, but at the same time he needed for his leg to heal. When his cousins had noticed it, he was on the brink of denying the injury. But he'd grown fearful and was glad now that his aunt was seeing to it.

As he thought of the current predicament, Artair's eyes became heavy. Whatever herbs had been boiled and given to him had begun to take effect.

IT WAS A chilly day and Glynis pulled her shawl tighter around her shoulders. She paced impatiently waiting for the right moment to again speak to Caelan. Once she put the matter to rest, it would be easier to decide what do to next.

With the bothersome issue of the apology and the kiss—no matter how light it was—she couldn't think straight enough to make a life-altering decision. Whether to accept Cait's offer to live there or to return to Keep Ross meant very different outcomes. She'd not been invited to remain with her aunt, though she was sure if she asked, she could stay indefinitely. The third option was to return to Barra and to her family.

Her father and mother's home was a bit larger than Cait's. Glynis studied the beautiful house for a moment. However, there was very little privacy with her parents, two brothers, one wife, and two bairns. There was also a small staff and various relatives and friends who visited regularly.

At Cait's home, life would be much more peaceful. Not only was life slower, but there was little chance she'd ever run into the men who'd attacked her and her brother, Gavin.

Gavin had always been her protector and guardian. Had he not followed her that fateful day she would probably have been raped and possibly taken away from her home forever by the men who'd accosted her.

Her brother had stopped the attackers. He had fought

valiantly, screaming for her to run whilst he remained there surrounded by men who ultimately left him for dead.

Despite his surviving the attack, a reminder of that day would forever remain. One side of his face was now scarred horribly, where one of the attackers had sliced across it. The slash went from beside his left eye, down past the side of his mouth to his chin. Gavin's handsome face was disfigured forever. And it was her fault.

Sometimes she wished he'd not rescued her. Despite his efforts to make her feel better by acting normal, it was clear to her that he was no longer the confident, cocky rogue he'd once been. And although women continued to be attracted to him, he hadn't shown interest in anyone since recovering.

"What are ye doing out here? Ye're shivering." Caelan appeared suddenly, catching her off guard.

Glynis hadn't noticed that while she'd been thinking about her brother, the shawl had slipped down her arms.

"I am waiting to speak to ye," she replied doing her best to appear unaffected by his proximity. Something about him sent her blood to race and caused heat to rise up from her chest to her face. "Ye and I must resolve an issue."

The absence of expression on his face was utterly annoying. Other than a slight flex at his jawline, he didn't seem to hear her.

Then he leaned his head to the side just a bit. "What issue?"

Glynis closed the distance between them. "Why did ye kiss me? Is that an English way of accepting an apology?"

With a soft chuckle, Caelan shook his head. "Ye are a persistent lass." He motioned to an alcove. "Get out of the weather."

Upon moving into the alcove, Glynis realized it was much too small. Barely enough space for two people to stand. There was but a hair's breadth between them.

"Now, let us resolve this once and for all. I was not raised in England. I was raised in Glasgow, which, if ye did not know, is in Scotland," Caelan said, his warm breath fanning across her face. The blue eyes darkened when meeting hers. "Are ye truly despondent over the apology?"

"I would not say despondent," Glynis replied. "More bothered. Ye have not accepted my apology and then ye kissed me. I need to make some decisions and it is best to not have anything clouding my mind."

His lips curved just enough that she noticed a deep dimple on his right cheek. "I do not feel that ye meant to hurt me, but that yer reaction was impulsive. Therefore, no need to apologize. Ye may go forward with a clear mind. I forgive ye for it."

Releasing a deep breath, Glynis slumped forward. Unfortunately, due to the proximity between them, her head hit his chest.

Caelan was utterly still. It was as if he were aware of her lack of control and feared another kick or such.

It was the first time—other than when he'd kissed her—that she had been this close to a man and fear had not enveloped her. Admittedly, her pulse did race. Though she had a feeling it wasn't from fear but from something just as mortifying.

She lifted her face up and without thought she took his face in her hands and pulled him down so that his lips met hers. This time the kiss was not at all soft. Instead, it was hard. Urgent. Passionate.

His mouth took hers with what could only be described as raw hunger. His lips moving over hers, teasing and licking until everything began to spin.

When his arms encircled her, her body was flush against him. Caelan's hands traveled over her back, pulling her closer yet.

On and on the kiss continued. His tongue seeking permission to pass her lips and she parted them gladly. Needing more. Seeking to taste him fully.

The sounds they made were interesting. Caelan's deep moans intertwining with her softer ones.

When his mouth moved from hers, Glynis wanted to protest until realizing what he did. Ever so slowly, he trailed his lips down the side of her jaw to nibble on her ear. Shivers traveled down her body and she gasped when his tongue darted into her ear. Never had she felt so much wonder.

Her fingernails dug into the soft fabric of his tunic when he continued to explore, his lips traveling down the side of her neck sending pulses of heat throughout her body. Glynis prayed he'd never stop, that he continued to make her feel as if they were the only two people in the entire world.

"Ugh," he expelled a long breath, pushing away.

Glynis gasped at the suddenness and gawked at him. His chest lifted and lowered rapidly; his breathing harsh as his eyes bored into hers.

"This should never have happened," he said in a low growl. "Never."

With an angry expression, his gaze moved over her face.

"Ye should put cold water on yer mouth. Yer lips are very swollen." With that he stalked away. Practically running from her.

"Oh, no. What have I done?" Glynis covered her face with both hands. "I am such a fool," she muttered softly. Not only had she made matters worse, but now she truly had to leave.

There was no other option. She could not face Caelan again after her wanton behavior.

She raced to the well and drew a bucket of water. When she cupped water in her hands and lifted it to her face, the cold water was like a slap across the cheeks. One she felt to deserve. Once she splashed water over her face, she looked around to ensure no one saw her.

Caelan stood next to the stables with his hands on his hips looking off into the distance. His breathing was still hard, but he seemed more at ease than she felt.

Just as she turned toward the house, he looked in her direction. Glynis pretended not to see him. Instead, she lifted her hands up to smooth her hair trying to ensure she did not look as disheveled as she felt when walking into the house.

Upon entering the house, the only person in the kitchen was her aunt, who was busy cutting potatoes. "We must make haste. See about putting the lentils into boiling water," she instructed.

Thankfully, her aunt did not bother studying her face. Glynis did as told, doing her best to keep turned away.

"Where is Cait?" she asked lightly.

"I believe she went out front. She is asking someone to go fetch Grace and Maisie, to help with the warriors who are to arrive later today."

Glynis' stomach sunk. Had Cait gone to the side of the house and seen her and Caelan? Although they were in the alcove, someone could have caught sight of them emerging.

"I must ask her something," Glynis said and hurried back out of the kitchen before her aunt could stop her.

Walking past the empty dining hall and front room, she went to the front door. Just outside were Cait and another man, she recalled being a Ross. An uncle named, Lyall.

Cait turned to her just as the man walked away. Her gaze instantly moving to her lips. "Ye should put a cold compress on yer lips. Lady Mariel will notice."

Instantly her face heated and Glynis covered it with both hands. "What was I thinking?"

Cait's lively laughter made her cringe. "One usually doesn't think during times like these. I am sure ye did not plan for the handsome Caelan to ravage ye."

"Shhh," Glynis hissed, but then gave up at Cait's amused expression. "I would say it was I who ravaged him."

"Oh, my." Cait took Glynis by the hand and led her back inside. "Come to my bedchamber, let us see what we can do."

Once ensconced in the privacy of the bedroom, Glynis let herself relax. "I am so embarrassed. What will I do? I must leave immediately. Make up an excuse to give Aunt Mariel and seek help…"

"Ye will not do any such thing," Cait said in a patient voice. "Everyone has lapses such as these. I am sure. An interlude does not mean either of ye are committed to making an abrupt decision."

Glynis was not convinced. They were to see one another time and again, surely it would be at the very least, awkward.

"I cannot pretend to be unaffected," she insisted. "How will I be able to face him?"

"Do not seek him out in private," Cait said, as if that were obvious. The house was not big enough to hide from anyone for long, not to mention they took meals together daily.

"Do yer best to stay away from him."

"I suppose I can try."

Her new confidant gave her an impish grin. "Is he a good kisser? I often wondered with him seeming so different from his brothers. Always in control."

Despite the dire situation, she found herself having to share. Glynis giggled. "I do not have much to compare him with. I must however confess to wishing the kissing to never end."

Glynis bit down on her lip to keep from smiling. "This is not a game. I am no longer a young lass without thought of consequences."

"True. However, we are still young and should enjoy things such as kisses."

"Not from a man who does not hide the fact that he doesn't like me."

For a moment, Cait considered her. The young woman then shook her head. "I would say quite the opposite. Caelan can barely keep from ye. It is very obvious by how often he steals looks at ye and the way he tracks yer movements upon entering a room."

"Do not say such things," Glynis said truly mortified. "I will feel ill at ease now."

Thankfully the men did not appear for last meal. The servants, Masie and Grace, as well as Cait's mother, arrived with a cartful of victuals and with the precision of seasoned performers began preparations for the meal.

Meanwhile outside, Stuart's uncle ordered the men about to build temporary shelters and places for bonfires and the like.

"One hundred is many men. I do believe they will bring their own cooks and provisions," her aunt Mariel told the women, who continued unfazed, counting out potatoes and onions and popping them into sacks.

"It never hurts to be prepared," Masie informed them giving Glynis a once over. Her gaze seemed to see past the exterior, but despite it Glynis liked her.

"Ye seem quite at ease with the task we face," she told the older woman who gave her a solid nod.

"I am. 'Tis many a time that a large Ross army camped in this region when at war with Clan Uisdein or Macdonald," Masie replied.

"I remember the warriors too well. Most of them kind and grateful for the hot meals in the winter," Grace added. "Some of the injured were kept in this very room just there." She pointed to the dining hall.

"There will be no injuries this time," Aunt Mariel stated. "They are only here to become familiar with the territory."

Glynis wondered if it was true. There was tension just under the surface during the last meal they'd had together. It was as if the men hid something. Perhaps there were intruders to be dispatched. Why was her cousin Darach sending so many men?

She slipped out to the dining hall and peeked into the front room. The only one there was Lyall, who slept in a chair. He didn't wake when she tiptoed past to Stuart's study.

The room was tidy, with only a few items on one side of the table. Spread in the center was a makeshift map with an area circled on the shoreline. Next to it was a note: *Campsites.*

At the sound of footfalls, Glynis jumped.

"What is that?" Cait walked up and looked down at the map.

"I do not know. I suspect, the men are hiding the fact that there are encroachers on the shoreline."

"Ah," Cait gave her a light shrug. "Aye, I know. Stuart is hoping to hide it from me, but he's not a good liar."

They hurried out when they heard someone clear their throat. Lyall was still in the chair and appeared to be waking. He yawned widely and gave them a questioning look.

"Were ye watching me sleep?"

Glynis shook her head. "We are walking through. We did not mean to wake ye."

"I am a very light sleeper," he replied, crossing his arms. A moment later his head fell forward, and a light snore sounded.

"How can he sleep like that?" Cait said walking to the dining hall.

BY THE TIME last meal began, the women were all convinced the men were hiding something. It was comical how everyone kept stealing glances and speaking in circles while trying to keep a conversation going.

"The guards should be arriving soon," Aunt Mariel said. "I suppose the expedition begins at dawn."

Stuart nodded. "Aye, we will split into three teams to better discover the routes."

"Where exactly will these routes converge?" Glynis asked, keeping her gaze purposefully away from Caelan.

"The shore north of the village," Caelan replied flatly.

"Will ye be back in time for last meal?" Cait asked. "We do not wish to prepare food only to have it go to waste."

The men exchanged looks and Glynis pressed her lips together to keep from laughing. It was serious business. The Ross men could face adversaries prepared to attack. However, in the moment, they were enjoying a light repose before the worry what would come the following day.

"We are preparing braised boar and potatoes with onion pies," her aunt continued. "We will be cooking all day."

"Simple porridge and bread in the morning," Grace, who walked up with a tray of cheese, added.

As long as she kept from looking at Caelan, it was possible to breathe normally. She couldn't eat. That was asking too much of her tense body. Instead, she sipped the honeyed mead and nibbled on a piece of bread, doing her best to remain calm.

"Are ye not hungry?" Caelan asked and she looked up to meet his gaze. The man had the audacity to look amused.

"I have an upset stomach. Must have eaten something rotten earlier."

"Oh, dear," her aunt said, patting her hand. "What did ye eat?"

Cait coughed, choking on whatever she was eating. Thankfully, it took everyone's attention so that she could glare at Caelan. His gaze moved to her lips and she gasped turning away to watch a red-faced Cait trying to compose herself.

Glynis blew out a breath. "I need some fresh air."

"Caelan, please accompany Glynis. A short walk will do wonders for her," her aunt said and sipped her mead. "I plan to relax and put my feet up. Tomorrow will be a busy day indeed," she continued.

Glynis leaned over and pressed a kiss to her aunt's cheek taking advantage to speak. "Why are ye asking him to walk with me?"

"Ye said ye needed to clear things up. This will be a perfect opportunity."

If Aunt Mariel only knew how much they'd cleared things up earlier.

CHAPTER SEVEN

THERE WASN'T ANY way to make an excuse and get out of walking with Glynis outside. As much as he'd enjoyed goading her a few moments earlier, he had made a vow to avoid her at all costs.

He looked to Artair; but unfortunately, his cousin was deep in conversation with Stuart and did not pay him any mind. There wasn't anyone else he could pawn Glynis off on, so he stood and walked to wait as she kissed her aunt.

She stood and barely glanced at him. "I must retrieve my shawl."

They walked out the back door, both purposely turning away from the back of the house where the alcove was.

He fell in step beside her. "Ye and the other women are aware of the true reason for our plans tomorrow." It was obvious by the questions the women had asked in an attempt to get them to admit it. Perhaps Stuart had not noticed, but he doubted it.

"Aye, I saw the map," Glynis said, practically admitting to going into Stuart's study.

"Ye should not go into a man's study unless invited."

She let out a breath. "Father has said the same thing to me. But I believe women should be privy to events that could affect our lives. Why do men persist in the thought we are oblivious creatures?"

"That is not something I would ever use to describe ye," Caelan admitted. "However, ye are impetuous and without regard for polite boundaries."

"Polite boundaries?" She whirled to face him. "Such as? Being ravaged by a deranged man in plain daylight?" Her eye blazed with fury, her lips twisted baring her teeth. He'd never seen such magnificent beauty.

Caelan threw his head back and laughed.

"Why are ye laughing? I am very serious."

He met her gaze unable to keep from smiling. "Aye, I know ye are. I believe it was ye who kissed me first and I laugh because ye never cease to surprise me."

Her cheeks pinkened. "Keeping ye entertained is not my reason for living." He watched her stalk away. The sun had already set. In the twilight, her red hair and fair skin seemed to glow. She hurried in the direction of the wheat field. She'd become lost in no time if continuing too far.

"Wait," Caelan called and ran after her. "There are always wild boars in the field, ye do not want to go there."

"Ye are trying to scare me. I know there are no wild boars this close to the house." The stubborn woman continued to the edge of the field, gave him a daring look, and strolled directly into the neatly planted rows.

"Why can ye not be calm or rational," he mumbled and walked in after her. He turned to his left and then right and she was nowhere to be seen.

"Glynis," he called out. "Stop acting like a child."

There was a sound that sounded like a snort and he held his breath listening intently. If it was a wild boar, Glynis was probably frozen in fear.

He pulled out a stalk from the ground and swung it to attract the animal's attention.

Suddenly he was grabbed from behind. He instinctively rounded, grabbed the offender around the midsection, and tossed them to the ground.

He could only gawk at seeing Glynis flat on her back. The wind knocked out of her.

"What are ye doing?"

"I…I…I…tried to..sc…scare ye." She let out a whoosh of air and scrambled to her feet.

"Ye did not scare me, but ye almost got yer neck broken. I wonder about ye Glynis," he said taking her by the shoulders and searching her arms and face to ensure she was unharmed.

She pushed him away. "I do not require an escort. I am going for a walk alone. Being around ye makes me act strange and distracts me."

"From?"

Her gaze met his. "What?"

"What am I distracting ye from?"

"I cannot think clearly when ye are around. And I do very stupid things. Like just now." She pulled her hair loose from its pins. The fiery tresses tumbled past her shoulder. "Now I have to fix my hair."

He followed her to a rock, where she sat and began threading her fingers through her hair then nimbly twisting it back into the usual bun at the nape of her neck. Once that was done, she stood and dusted her skirts.

"Should we address what happened earlier?" Caelan wasn't sure why he brought it up. Probably because he also could not think clearly when around the perplexing lass.

Glynis looked at him. Her expression incredulous. "No. Absolutely not."

"Ye want me and do not know how to keep from thinking about me. About how my kisses make ye feel." As he spoke, Caelan moved closer to her. "Ye will relive it tonight, in bed."

She held her ground, but the reddening of her cheeks gave away just how much he affected her. Caelan should have stopped, should have paused to think. Instead, he closed the distance and bent until their faces almost touched. "Admit it. Ye want me as much as I want ye."

He'd not meant to say so much, but the words left his lips before he realized what he'd said. The lass' chest lifted and lowered with each breath, taking his attention from her face. The tops of her creamy breasts had also pinkened at his words. Would her entire body be as rosy when he ravaged her?

"Ye do not know anything," she finally said. "I am not interested in ye or any man for that matter. What I wish is to live alone, in a quiet place and to be at peace." She took a step back and crossed her arms.

A bark of laughter escaped. "The last thing ye need is a solitary life. Ye would not stand it for longer than a few days. Ye are, and will always be, a troublesome fiery lass."

Her expression became pensive, it was as if he said something that made her think about something unpleasant. When she blinked, he saw that her eyes had misted. Her throat shifted as she swallowed.

"I am troublesome, which is why ye should keep away. No one deserves to be tied to the likes of me."

When she raced into the field again, this time he didn't

follow. There weren't any wild boar about, that he knew of. He'd just said it to annoy her. Hopefully she would not become terribly lost.

The sounds of hooves were followed by a slight ground tremble. The warriors arrived.

HE'D NEVER GROW used to the sight of so many armed men mounted and prepared for battle. If the women in the house did not suspect what was truly happening, one look at the warrior army and they'd know.

Caelan hurried to meet Stuart and Artair as they stood in front of the house prepared to greet the men.

He was surprised when Darach dismounted. It was rare that a laird would accompany his guardsmen for a trivial circumstance. However, when Darach rushed to Stuart and hugged him, it was evident he missed his brother and wished to spend time with him.

The laird stood tall, his golden mane pulled back and tied with a strap. Caelan walked to him. "Ye cannot go with us."

Darach's hazel gaze challenged when meeting his. "Since when do ye order me about?"

"We have no idea what to expect. The scouts we sent have not returned. And it is past time. They were either killed or captured. There is no time to waste, we must go at dawn—"

"Who did ye send?" Darach asked interrupting.

Stuart told him the names of the men. They were well-practiced scouts that had worked for the family for many years.

Darach's gaze narrowed. "I do not expect either of them to be caught easily."

"Unless they were expected," Stuart said in a low voice. "We have men working here that I've only met since arriving. I am sure some remain loyal to the last constable."

Darach motioned to the men still mounted and Stuart addressed them. "Temporary shelter for the night has been built over there." He pointed to the land behind the stables. "The evening meal will be served shortly." Stuart motioned to the space next to the house. There were benches set up where the men could sit and eat. Most would have to hold their bowls in their hands as there were only a few tables.

Artair, who was not limping as badly as he had been, took over. Showing the guards where the horses were to be kept. Feed had already been set out for the animals as well as troughs of water.

Caelan, Darach, and Stuart walked inside. Soon the leader of the archers and lead warrior also joined them. They went to the dining hall and sat around a table.

Stuart placed the map they'd drawn up on the table and they went over the logistics of the land.

"Since my scouts have not returned, we are not sure about the possibility of traveling in three directions and joining up at this point." Caelan pointed to the circle where the encroachers had been spotted.

Masie and Grace came out with cups of ale.

No sooner did they take a sip than the scouts appeared. The men looked tired and dirty.

Caelan asked for them to be brought food and drink and the men began explaining how treacherous the routes were to reach where the camp had been set up. Apparently, there was but one easy way to approach on horseback and it was impossible not to be seen.

"Very well thought out," Darach said. "What of the northern route. Why can't we reach them using it?"

One of the scouts shook his head. "Ye can, but there are no clear roads. Ye would have to go by bìrlinn. Otherwise, it is slow going. I managed to reach the shore but could not get close enough to see more than a few men."

They watched as the man began to draw the different routes they'd tried with success. When finding a good route, they'd had to approach on foot so as not to get caught.

They drew the best three routes. The southern one, the easiest. The northern one, the most treacherous.

"Where is Glynis?" Aunt Mariel entered and upon seeing Darach walked closer. The laird stood and kissed his mother.

Both turned to look at Caelan for his response. "I left her over by the field upon seeing the men arrive. She should be about here somewhere."

"Find her," his aunt said without care that he was in the middle of something. "Then ye can return to yer battle plan or whatever ye think requires so many men. I need her to help, we have many mouths to feed." With that, she stormed off.

"I'll return shortly," Caelan stood and stalked from the room. It wasn't his responsibility to keep track of the temperamental lass. She was probably hiding in the field waiting to attempt to scare him again for all he knew.

He was annoyed. He didn't have time for her foolishness when there was so much to do. In the morning, he, along with the Ross men, would go into a situation that they had no idea what the outcome would be. The scouts had spotted about twenty men, but they could not get closer to get a better assessment.

He searched the field but didn't see Glynis. Then upon seeing a man standing behind the stables, he went toward him.

The man, who worked with horses waved him closer. "A pair of the field workers approached the lass. She became very agitated and now refuses to budge from behind there."

Caelan met the man's gaze. "Why did no one come to fetch one of us?"

The man shrugged. "It just happened. I sent the men away thinking they were bothering her, but now see she is very upset."

"I will speak to her." Caelan walked around the corner unprepared for what he saw. Curled in a ball, Glynis covered her head and was sobbing.

He crouched down and kept his distance. "Glynis ye must stop at once. Stepmother needs ye to help with the food." His own mother had such fits after being robbed when returning from the village. It was obvious something of the like had happened to Glynis.

When she lifted her tear-streaked face, he met her gaze without emotion. It was the last thing she needed, to see her pain reflected. Anguish emanated from her.

"I cannot move. I am so sorry. I should never have come. Nothing will help me get over it. Will it?"

The question was a cry for reassurance.

"Ye will get past this, but it will happen slowly." Caelan let out a breath. "After my first battle, I could not sleep for days. I kept seeing the faces of the dead. One of them was a man I grew up with. I felt responsible for his death. Still do. I should have fought harder, protected him."

Glynis was riveted, her eyes never leaving his face. "What did ye do?"

"Accepted that it happened and that nothing I do can change the past."

Her eyes fell and she held out her hand. "I need to go help Aunt Mariel."

As soon as he assisted Glynis to stand, she rounded him and hurried in the direction of the house. Caelan followed but did not close the distance. One thing he knew was that when one felt guilty, it was a heavy burden that no other person could lift.

THE NEXT MORNING, it was still dark as everyone mounted. Darach refused to remain behind, so he, along with Caelan and Stuart, were to ride with the three separate groups. Caelan and twenty men would go north and try to navigate the inlets and find a way to reach the shore.

Stuart to the south with sixty men and Darach's group would be in the center.

"For the Clan!" Darach called out as the groups split and headed in the directions they'd planned. It would take four hours at least to reach their goal.

The closer to the shore they came, the faster his blood rushed. Caelan studied the grim expressions of his companions, noting the path ahead was indeed as the scouts had described it. Several men dismounted to slash a path for the horses to go fourth. Finally, when they could see the shore, they held back for a moment to ensure not to be seen.

From the slight elevation, they spotted a line of bìrlinns along the coast. Whoever the men were, they had a way to escape.

"I do not know what they plan. If twenty men came in each bìrlinn, it means there are at least eighty on shore," Caelan told one of the warriors.

"Aye, we cannot approach until the others arrive," the warrior replied.

Arrows flew in their direction and the warrior fell from his horse. Another one grunted and fell as well. Caelan and the others dismounted and rushed to shelter behind trees and bushes. He crawled to the moaning man with the arrow impaled on the right side of his chest and dragged him behind a tree.

"Bastards," an archer said, his keen gaze searching the area.

Their horses shuffled in a circle protecting them, by putting themselves at risk. Caelan watched his horse praying the beautiful animal would not be struck. Thankfully, the attackers did not strike the horses.

"They want our mounts," Caelan whispered. He reached up with his sword and hit his horse on the rump. The animal would instinctively run back in the direction of where they came and hopefully not be captured.

When the others did the same, the horses stampeded away. Men appeared and tried to catch the animals, giving Caelan and his men an opportunity to attack.

With the clang of swords, the smell of blood, and the fast movements, a battle commenced. The sounds of grunts, metal clanging, and men's screams filled the air.

Caelan swung his sword in a zigzag pattern, dispatching

man after man as they seemed to grow in number. Whoever they were they had been expecting them, seeming to know they'd be the smaller party.

The loud whines of horses told him that several of the mounts had been captured. One man mounted his, and Caelan almost smiled knowing the man would not be able to handle the angry beast.

As he sliced across a man's midsection and then turned to stab another, he whistled to his mount. Immediately the animal lifted up to his hindquarters, its huge hooves raking in the air. The unsuspecting rider fell, hitting the ground with such force, he was knocked unconscious.

The horse kicked its hind legs and trotted into the middle of the battle. A warhorse trained to fight, it moved sideways blocking men from one another, whether friend or foe.

Out of the corner of his eye, Caelan caught sight of a sword coming down and he barely had time to block it, the clash of the swords sending vibrations down his tiring arms.

And then it happened, what he both welcomed and feared. His entire body became rigid one second and the next it was as if his mind separated from it.

Filled with a burst of energy, he bent and picked up a dead man's sword and fought like a madman. Swinging both weapons with well-practiced precision, he felled first two, then four, and finally six men. Several gave him wide birth, seeming to be entranced by his movement.

A loud furious growl erupted as he raced to where one of his men fought two and within moments both lay on the ground.

The attackers that were left fled along with several of their horses.

Caelan could barely calm as he rushed to where the man who'd fallen from the horse came to. He grabbed the man's hair, lifting his head from the ground.

"Who are ye? Why are ye on our lands?" He shook the man, who grimaced and swung to punch him and missed.

Caelan's fist smashed into the man's jaw and the man looked about to pass out again.

"Who are ye?" Caelan repeated. "Speak." He laid his sword along the man's throat.

"I was hired for my sword and care not what happens to 'im," the man sputtered. "Name is McInerny, he hired us to come and fight for what he says is his land."

Cairn McInerny, of course. The bastard had returned with a hired army.

"How many?"

The man's eyes glazed over, but he managed to talk. "About sixty of us. Paid silver." The man passed out again and Caelan dropped his head.

The sounds of another battled sounded.

"Ye and ye," Caelan said motioning to two men. "See about the injured."

He pointed to another, who lived on Stuart's lands. "Ride to the village on my horse, see about a cart and another horse." He studied the man for a second. "He is temperamental but will behave if ye are stern with him."

He and the remaining men rushed to the shoreline to make their way to where the others fought.

It seemed the men were not as loyal as the ones who'd attacked Caelan's group, because upon seeing the number of warriors who appeared, they quickly surrendered.

The newly arrived encroachers and their injured were ushered to the boats. The dead buried.

Once the bìrlinns were out of sight, they turned their attention to Ross warriors who were injured and to a pair of men who they'd captured and would keep for questioning.

The two men they captured were the ones giving orders, so they were probably the ones who'd been hired by Cairn and tasked with forming the small army.

Swords for hire were rarely a loyal lot and soon the men told them everything they needed to know.

Cairn hired them and asked that they recruit men who would fight for coin. Unfortunately, the men were not aware of where Cairn was.

"If he distracted us to come here, then perhaps he and others could be on the opposite shore," Stuart said.

"Or the southern shore, in the direction he went," Caelan said, his stomach sinking at the thought. Clan Ross had a thriving village on the southern shore. His mother lived near there. If any harm came to her, he would skin Cairn McInerny alive.

"If I were him," Stuart said. "I would cause a distraction with my ultimate goal in mind. What does he wish for more than anything?"

"To be laird," Darach replied.

Stuart shook his head. "Aye, but that is not possible. I believe he wishes to hurt us for taking any chance of it from him."

"Go back to the house!" Darach screamed, running full speed toward his horse. "I will kill the bastard myself."

"Stepmother," Caelan said as realization dawned. Of course, Cairn had purposely caused several distractions. Part of it was to find out where exactly Mariel Ross was. She was the one unifying factor for all of them. If she were killed, none of them would withstand it.

As they galloped toward the house with about sixty men, Caelan looked to Stuart. "How many men are there to defend the women?"

His half brother's face was ashen. Not only was his mother threatened, but also his pregnant wife.

Caelan's fury rose.

"Ten. Perhaps five more. Most of them are not fighters, but workers."

It would be hours before they arrived. Unfortunately, the horses were showing signs of tiring and slowing.

Men on fresh horses rode up and upon Stuart's order, exchanged horses with them, so that the brothers could continue at full speed.

The first thing they saw was smoke in the distance. It was possible the attackers had set the house on fire.

Stuart growled, his face a mask of rage.

Upon arriving, there were several men rushing on foot around the house, Caelan signaled to a couple of warriors and they guided their horses to follow.

It was only moments before the intruders lay dead on the ground.

The six guards, their Uncle Lyall, and Artair fought against a group of men. Caelan directed his horse to the center of the battle using it as a batting ram, sending men jumping out of the way to keep from being trampled. Taking advantage, he jumped from the horse and quickly dealt with three, then fought a fourth, and within moments he too lay dead.

"Behind ye!" someone yelled, he thought it was Glynis. He turned swinging his sword and sliced a man across the chest. The man's eyes bulged before he flopped onto the ground.

Rain began to fall in earnest, the deluge adding a layer of chaos to the day.

"Give up now!" Darach called out and after just a few more attempts to defend, the intruders dropped their swords and lowered to their knees.

Caelan walked to the opposite side to ensure no one ran off.

"I will kill her and there is nothing any of ye can do about it," A man appeared dragging their mother. "Ye will watch her die, her blood will spill for yer mistreatment of Cairn McInerny. Ross brothers, ye must pay for—"

Lady Mariel screamed and shuffled sideways as the man's head rolled past her foot. His body collapsed onto the ground behind her, a pool of blood forming from the gaping wound that was his neck.

"I did not wish to hear any more of what he had to say," Caelan said walking up to the severed head and giving it a swift kick. "Never threaten my family."

Stuart rushed into the house seeking out Cait, and Darach saw to his mother ensuring she was unharmed.

For a long moment, Caelan stood with his head hung down focusing on the growing red stain being washed away by the rain.

His chest heaved with each breath. Dragging his sword, he staggered to the side of the house and fell against the wall.

"Ye saved her life." Glynis stood in front of him, her hair plastered to her face from the pelting rain.

"How is she?" Caelan asked, not daring to look up. He knew what he'd done was monstrous. Taking someone's life and then kicking the severed head. However, when fury filled him, he could not control it.

"Worried about ye. She asked that I come speak to ye and assure ye she is well and very proud of ye."

"Proud?" He looked up and met her gaze. "What do ye think?"

"That if ye had been there when I was attacked my brother would be unharmed and the attackers dead."

Her honesty startled him. "Ye do not think me a monster?"

Pushing her wet hair from her face, she shook her head. "No. I think that yer calm façade is a cover for the fiery man beneath. As ye are aware, I too have a temperament that I do a horrible job of hiding. I understand it."

Caelan closed his eyes and let out a breath and then a second one. With each exhalation, he released the pent-up fury that sizzled under his skin until he felt as if he might collapse from exhaustion.

"Let us go inside," Glynis said. "I am a wee bit wet." She lifted her soaking wet skirts and released them to flop past her ankles.

They walked side by side into the house and were immediately greeted by red-nosed Maisie who hurried him into his bedchamber. "Remove yer clothes before ye catch yer death. I will get ye a hot bath as soon as the tub is available," Maisie said with a loud sniff. "Ye and yer brothers arrived just in time to save us."

"No need. I am fine," he replied wanting nothing more than to collapse on the bed and not have to speak to anyone. "I need to sleep."

Just as he entered the bedchamber, Grace hurried in and placed a plate on the table next to the bed. "Have ye a bit to eat and drink. The mead is heated to warm ye up."

"What about the fire? Is the house harmed?"

Masie shook her head. "The rain put it out, thank God. Only one of the back rooms is damaged."

After the women walked out, Caelan lay naked on the bed wrapped in a blanket. He managed to drink down the mead but ignored the food.

CHAPTER EIGHT

IT WAS STILL the next morning. The men outside barely making a sound. But she'd seen them patrolling when first getting up.

Glynis walked through the dining room considering what needed to be done to start the morning meal preparations.

Everyone had been up late. It was hard for everyone to settle after what happened. They'd sat around the tables talking and going over all the events of the day. It was as if everyone needed reassurance. Even Caelan had come out after a while and joined the conversation.

There had been a collective relief when Caelan had killed the man who'd held her aunt with a blade at her throat.

However, the man who wished them ill remained alive and they had no idea where he was. They were awaiting news before going in search of the man, Cairn.

In the kitchen, her aunt and Clara were the only ones there. At hearing her name, Glynis stopped and listened.

"She is very impetuous," her aunt said. "She's been through a lot, so we must be patient with her."

Clara sighed audibly. "Perhaps it would be best for her to return to Bara after all is settled."

"Perhaps," her aunt replied.

Glynis could not blame them. She had done nothing but

cause her aunt constant worry.

"Glynis, what are ye doing up so early?" her aunt said when she walked into the kitchen. "Ye should be resting."

She turned and smiled. "It is ye who should be in bed still. Ye had a trying day."

"Nonsense," her aunt said with a firm shake of her head. "I had no doubt that my sons would see to my safety. Either Stuart would have speared him with an arrow, or that berserker stepson of mine would do what he did."

She couldn't keep from chuckling. "Berserker? He does seem to lose control when battling."

"Aye, it is the only time." Her aunt went in search of the wooden box Caelan kept his tea in. "I am becoming used to his tea in the morning. Let us find some."

"Ye must see if ye can find the one he said to have gifted ye," Glynis told her. "Aunt Mariel. I think I will spend the day in my bedchamber. I will take some food and ale so I can remain cloistered. I find that I need time of reflection and rest."

Her aunt gave her a curious look. "I heard ye were upset the other day. Is that what this is about?"

"Aye," she replied truthfully, adding. "I must find a way to fight the fear inside, once and for all. I have also decided to return home."

"Do not make decisions in haste," her aunt replied. "We have just gotten past this attack. Let's take time to rest."

The next few days went by without incident. Glynis kept busy helping with chores and once they were completed, she retreated to her room to avoid Caelan.

She could not stop thinking about the conversation between her aunt and Clara. She did need to return to Bara. Not only because she was a bother, but also because she needed to face her fears. And she had to speak to her brother about what happened and together do what they could to find the men and ensure they were punished.

ONE MORNING GLYNIS woke up with her mind made up. She would return home. There was no need to bother her family with it. Instead, she would do it on her own.

"How fare ye?" Glynis said strolling into the kitchen and as usual finding her aunt there.

While her aunt boiled water and busied herself with making tea. Glynis took a chunk of leftover bread, some cheese, and dried meat and placed it in the center of a large cloth. She then walked to the door hiding the bundle in the folds of her skirt. "I will check on getting eggs so Maisie and Grace can prepare them for breakfast."

She walked to the chicken pen and placed her food bundle there. Then gathered eggs.

An hour later, Glynis hurried to the corrals and found a mare that seemed docile.

"What can I do for ye, miss?" A young lad appeared.

"I require a small cart and horse. I am going to visit a friend."

While the lad did as he was told, she kept an eye out. But no one was about, it was much too early.

Finally, she climbed onto the bench of the cart and looked at the boy. "Do not disturb anyone, if they ask if ye have seen me, tell them I have gone to the village to visit Bree."

The lad frowned and nodded. "Aye, miss."

She guided the mare away from the house, around the back of the stables, toward the road. Once there she would go in the direction opposite the village and south to the shore. It would be easy enough to hire a seat on one of the bìrlinns to Bara from there. She would also pay someone to return the horse and cart to Keep Ross.

Glynis had left a note for her aunt so she would not worry and asked that no one come after her. It was best for her to move on and not continue hiding. Otherwise, her fears would never be gone.

It wasn't until several hours later that she stopped looking over her shoulder. Her aunt must have told everyone she needed rest and not to bother her.

It was a long time later that she began to wonder what to do when night came. Perhaps find an inn or a place to hide and sleep. In her hurry to get away, she'd not considered how to protect herself from rain or such. Other than her thick cloak and scarf, she'd not been able to get any blankets. She looked over her shoulder into the tiny cart. There was a small bag of feed for the horse and her bundle of food. That was it.

"Ugh." She blew out a breath. Thankfully, although downcast, there didn't seem to be any rain clouds in the sky.

This was a different path than the one they'd used to come to the house. Thankfully, she was a good navigator and knew enough to stick to the shoreline and the roads would lead to a coastal village she was familiar with. Unfortunately, she wasn't sure how far before she arrived at a village where she could seek shelter.

It was late in the day when she finally stopped to relieve herself and reassess the situation. In the distance, the call of the seabirds as they found a place to nest for the night echoed around her. The dimming light sent long eerie shadows that stretched across the ground like tendrils of gloom. The wind thankfully remained gentle, but at the same time colder as the day ended.

Climbing back onto the bench, Glynis urged the horse to continue forth. There had to be a village nearby. People made lives near the seashore, fishing for a living and such. Other than a lone cottage however, she didn't see much.

Deciding to take a chance that the cottage was as deserted as it looked, she guided the horse towards it. Moments later, she almost cried in relief when discovering that other than a table and a lopsided chair, the tiny cottage was indeed abandoned.

Hurriedly, she settled the horse beside the cottage in a ramshackle shelter that, despite one side of the roof drooping, would provide a reprieve from any rain and cold wind. The mare was sweet-natured and seemed pleased with the portion of oats she was given, and the water Glynis had fetched from the nearby creek.

Once that was complete, she refilled the small bucket from the creek and went into the cottage. Then she foraged for branches and sticks to start a fire. Her pile of wood was plentiful, and she hoped it would last the entire night until she left in the morning.

She eyed it and then went back out and collected more, just in case.

Finally, feeling exhausted she used a thick branch to bar the door. Within moments a cheery fire warmed the room. Glynis settled onto a spot in the floor she swept with a broken broom and let out a breath. She'd drank water from the creek and then ate some of the bread and dry meat she'd brought. Hopefully, the next day she'd reach the southern shore and be headed home.

Hard rainfall woke Glynis. She lay next to the fire bundled in her cloak. The sounds of the wind and rain were startling. She added more wood to the fire and prayed the rain would stop when the sun rose.

As if in reply, the wind rattled the small cottage and water dripped from the roof into the house. Drip after drip onto the floor. Thankfully it was on the opposite side of where she lay. She got up and placed the bucket under the drip to keep the water from pooling further.

"Goodness," she murmured and eyed the chair. One leg had broken off and she wondered if there was a way to fix it and sit at the table.

Since she was awake, she worked on the chair, managing to slip the broken leg back into the hole and banging on it with a branch until it was set. Then she tested it. Gingerly sitting down until feeling secure.

"Ha!" she called out, proud of her accomplishment. She then pulled the bundle of food closer to inspect what was left. Half a chunk of bread and an apple. Not much, but enough for another day. She had coin and could purchase food upon reaching a village.

All that needed to happen was for the rain to stop.

UNFORTUNATELY, THE RAIN had still not abated by late morning the next day. She hurried out to feed the horse and ensure it was as dry as possible and returned inside soaked and freezing as she'd not worn her cloak to ensure it didn't get wet.

After securing the door, she dragged the chair and table closer to the fire. Glynis then set a long branch from over the back of the chair to the top of the table.

She peeled the wet clothes off and placed them over the branch to dry. Then she donned her chemise she'd left inside and sat next to the fire.

The rain continued as she began pacing. Her clothes remained damp, but it mattered little as she could not go anywhere.

Blowing out a breath she wiped the grimy window and looked out. A face appeared and she jumped away, a scream tearing from her.

Pounds on the door made her jump.

"Open the damn door," Caelan shouted over the storm.

For a moment, she considered telling him to go away. However, he could easily kick the door in, and the cold would permeate quickly.

She trudged to the door and tugged the branch free so that the door would open. He stormed into the cottage, a ball of wetness and fury.

In that moment, she feared him much more than the storm and glanced past him. If she ran, perhaps she could reach the horse. He would be a bit encumbered by the wet clothing.

"Do not think about it. I will hunt ye down and return ye to my aunt trussed up like a prize hog."

Her eyes widened. "Ye would not dare."

"Do not test me in this."

She let out a breath. "Please close the door, ye are allowing the cold air in."

Once he shut the door and used the branch to fasten it, he glared at her. "My stepmother is sick with worry because of ye."

"I—I need to do something. I left her a note so she would not fret."

When he took a deep breath, she fortified herself for what he'd do next. "Ye riding out into a storm right after an attack is no reason to worry, then?"

Glynis hung her head. "I must go back. Help avenge what happened to my brother. Ye wouldn't understand..." She stopped when he closed the distance between them, his jaw clenched.

"Stop speaking," he ordered through clenched teeth.

For what seemed like an eternity, Caelan held her gaze, seeming to see through her every thought and excuse she was attempting to formulate.

When he stalked back to the door, she let out a shaky breath.

"Has yer horse been fed?"

"Aye, I brought oats with me. She's eaten twice already. And I have a bucket collecting rainwater for whatever else is needed."

"Ye can hang yer clothes here. To dry," she said, removing her clothes from the drying rack she'd fashioned with a branch and the chair.

Silently his gaze traveled over her. It was then she realized she stood before him in nothing more than a sheer chemise.

"Oh, goodness," she exclaimed holding her clothes up to cover herself.

He huffed seemingly unimpressed and went to the fireplace. After placing more wood into the fire, he draped his sopping wet cloak over the chair.

Taking advantage of his turned back, Glynis hurriedly pulled her shift on, deciding to leave the dress and skirts off since they remained damp.

His thick belt landed on the floor with a thud and then Caelan struggled to remove the soaked tunic up over his head. Once that was done, he draped it over the branch and sat down to remove his boots and stockings next. She stared without blinking and wondered if he was going to take his breeches off as well.

"I know ye want to say something," Glynis began. "I should explain the reason I left."

"Do not speak right now," he spat each word out past gritted teeth. "I do not have the patience for it."

With an annoyed grunt, he managed to remove the rest of his clothing, placing his breeches and stockings over the same branch.

He walked closer to the fire naked as the day he was born.

Glynis stood rooted to the spot. He was magnificent; beautifully made, and by the tension that emanated, very, very angry.

"My cloak is dry," she croaked. "It is there." She pointed when he turned. That he'd not bothered to cover himself was either because he did not care, or he was too furious to realize what he did.

Allowing her gaze to trail from his broad shoulders to the expanse of his back, Glynis could scarcely believe how lucky she was to study his form. The back tapered to a trim waist and lower to what she could only describe as a delectable bottom. His thighs were muscular, a testament to his constant riding.

When he turned to reach for the cloak, she averted her gaze despite the incredible surge of curiosity.

There was a loud clap of thunder and Glynis peered up at the ceiling. She hated that the horses were outside exposed to the weather because of her.

"We will leave as soon as the storm passes," Caelan said looking out the small window.

Glynis made a small pallet with her skirts as close as she could to the hearth. The fire emanated good heat and she was glad for it.

"I hope we have enough wood. Otherwise, what will we do for warmth?" she asked in a low voice.

Over his shoulder, Caelan gave her a bored look and stalked across the room to where a pile of dilapidated items remained. He rummaged through it finding a broken stool, a collapsed basket, and what looked to be the remains of a wooden bowl. "This should be enough to see us through the night."

The night. Glynis let out a breath. He was right, by the sounds of the weather outside, the storm would not calm for a while.

He placed the items next to the hearth and blew out a breath. "Thank ye for the cloak," he said sounding calmer. "I am sure to present an interesting picture."

Glynis was too distraught to do more than smile. Indeed, he looked ridiculous. The cloak only fell to just above his knees. But in a way, with the mused hair and lack of proper attire, he was more approachable.

"I am sorry," Glynis said wrapping her arms around her knees. "I have made a mess of things. Again."

"What exactly did ye plan to do once arriving in Barra?"

Glynis bit her bottom lip, her eyes misting. "I do not know for sure. All I know is that I have to do something to tear this guilt out. It is like a weight that does not allow me to breathe. I hate what happened."

"What exactly happened?" His gaze locked with hers. "Tell me."

Glynis tore her eyes from his and stared into the fire. "I wanted to go visit a friend, who just had her first bairn. My father would only allow me to go if one of my brothers escorted me. I asked Gavin, the younger one, and he said he could not until the next day." Glynis closed her eyes remembering his face before the attack.

"Go on."

"I left anyway. It was not that far, and I thought the walk would be pleasant as the weather that day was unusually warm. About halfway there, three men appeared. They grabbed me, demanded I give them coin. When I only produced a meager amount, they became angry and began tearing my clothes away."

When she hesitated, Caelan nodded. "Yer brother came then?"

She nodded. "Aye, they did not do much more than toss me about. It was as if they thought it a great game to terrorize me. Then Gavin appeared and everything changed. He screamed for me to run. I should have stayed and helped him. They beat him mercilessly and left him on the side of the road."

"I must punish them for what they did, leaving my brother

damaged, his face scarred…" She closed her eyes as tears spilled down her cheek. Moments later she was sobbing uncontrollably, unable to catch her breath.

Then she was in Caelan's arms, tightly held as she continued to cry. "Why do I keep doing such foolish things. It is as if I am compelled to run headfirst without regard for how my actions affect others. What if ye would have been attacked? I would never have forgiven myself."

Caelan lifted her chin so that she could look at him. "I will help ye. But first, ye must calm."

Her eyes fell closed at the warmth of his body against hers. Caelan had to be cold, but his skin felt hot. Possibly because he'd been standing so close to the fire.

It was not a shock, but more of an expectation when his mouth closed over hers. They would make love; she was sure of it. And once again, she dove headfirst without consideration of any consequences.

It wasn't the first time Glynis was intimate with a man, however it felt as if this was new, something she'd never be the same after. The feel of his skin as she skimmed her hands over it was intoxicating.

In between kisses, he removed her clothes. First the shift and then the chemise leaving her bare to him.

Again, his mouth took hers with wild abandon, kissing her with the desperation of a man who'd not been with a woman in a long time. Had he not?

Pressed against him, her body hummed at the promise of more pleasure to come. She wrapped her leg around his hips as they lay side to side, needing to be closer yet and sending a clear message that they would not stop at only a kiss.

Caelan pushed her onto her back and came over her, he

lifted and studied her face for a moment. "Ye are the most beautiful woman I've ever kissed."

She wanted to believe it was true. It felt true. But the ever-present lack of trust reared for an instant. Once his mouth took hers again and the full weight of him claimed her, she could only think in the moment.

Trailing his lips down the side of her neck, Glynis gasped when his mouth closed over her right breast and he suckled at her nipple teasing it with his teeth. Fire coursed through her veins, pooling at the center of her being.

She raked her fingers across his shoulders and then through his hair. Lost in the sensations, as he trailed his lips to the opposite breast, Glynis could only moan when he repeated the process sucking the taut tip into his mouth with greed.

Just as she began to grow impatient, needing more, his hand slid up from her thigh to between her legs.

Glynis let out a shaky moan at his touching her in the most intimate place. His fingers slid between the folds and then with the pad of one, he circled the sensitive nub.

"Oh!" Glynis cried out. Never had she been touched so intimately. The threat of coming undone just by a man's touch was new to her. "What are ye doing?"

Just as she started to ask another question, once again his mouth covered hers, tongue delving past her lips swallowing any more words. At the same time, he pushed a finger into her body, sending ripples of pleasure through her.

Glynis cried out as a hard release exploded from her and she clutched his hand with hers, not wanting him to remove it, not yet. First, she had to settle.

"Ye are not finished," Caelan whispered pulling both of her

hands over her head and then holding them in place with one of his.

"Ye are to reach climax again and again."

Her eyes widened. Was it possible? Once again, his hand covered her sex, his nimble fingers teasing until she could barely withstand it. He released her hands and lowered until his face was between her legs.

Glynis' eyes rolled back when his mouth took her, his tongue delving into where his fingers had been and then flicking up to tease the already sensitive nub.

"Oh. Oh." She repeated over and over, as everything threatened to disappear. "Ye. I want ye," she stammered. "Caelan please…"

He lifted and looked up meeting her gaze. "Are ye sure?"

"Yes. Please. Ye must."

He straightened. On his knees, he wrapped his hand around the shaft and she could not keep from watching as the thick head protruded from the end of his fist. It was as if he assured himself of what to do next.

With a primitive growl, he came over her. Guiding himself to her entrance with one quick thrust he was fully seated.

Both released a cry at the same time, then as she began to settle, he moved in a rhythmic steady pace that drove her past insanity.

Straightening his arms, he drove into her time and again, the pace faster and harder as his entire body became drenched in perspiration. His gaze locked with hers for a long moment and Glynis was lost in them.

Everything went out of focus moments later. A loud moan escaping as what felt like a gust of heat blew her away. She stiffened, unable to do more than clutch Caelan's shoulders, lost in the most wonderful sensations she'd ever experience.

CAELAN COULDN'T STOP. He'd convinced himself he'd only tease her, bring her to climax, and then take care of himself.

Lost in her now, he could not imagine stopping. His body screamed for release, but he did not allow it. It was much too wonderful an experience to put a stop to it. For months he'd kept from the tavern, kept from being with women to think clearer and save himself for someone important.

He was glad for it as this experience with Glynis drove him to the brink of madness. He had to stop, had to allow release. Already Glynis was climbing again, and he knew it was too much for her. It would be her fourth release and she would be tender after.

Sliding his hands under her bottom, he lifted her to give him deeper access. Lost in the moment, red hair spread around her, lips parted, and hands clutching the cloak she lay upon, Glynis was like a goddess.

Heat pooled between his legs and Caelan threw his head back, thrusting once, twice, and then finding a release so all-consuming his entire body shuddered uncontrollably.

It was impossible to move, to remove himself from her. All he could do was lay over her as she kissed his temples and pulled something over them. Her skirts perhaps.

HEAT ENVELOPED HER and Glynis snuggled closer to the source. Soon she'd have to get up and dress. She inhaled deeply wondering how much wood Caelan had put into the hearth to create so much heat.

Letting out a deep breath, she opened her eyes. Caelan laid facing her, his face calm, but shiny with perspiration. At first, she wondered if they lay too close to the fire, then realization dawned. He was feverish.

"Caelan," she whispered shaking him. "Ye are unwell."

"Mmmm." He didn't open his eyes.

"Wake up, we must return and find a healer." Glynis shook him, but it was of no avail.

She got up and dressed in a hurry. Then she got his tunic and breeches. After much struggle, she managed to dress him, not bothering with his boots. There was no time to lose.

Leaving him wrapped in her cloak, she took his still damp one and hurried outside. Thankfully, although the day was quite cloudy, it had stopped raining.

She pulled the cart to the front of the house, then hitched his horse to it. She would tether her mare to the back once she found a way to get Caelan onto it.

Finally, she was able to get Caelan onto the cart. Dragging him with her cloak and then somehow coaxing him awake long enough to climb onto the back. He'd once again fallen asleep as soon as he was on it.

She covered him with both cloaks and then climbed onto the bench. Looking up at the sky, she wiped away tears that poured freely.

"Please do not let him die. Not because of me."

Glynis snapped the reins and Caelan's warhorse broke into a gallop. She looked over her shoulder and noted that the mare was able to keep up.

CHAPTER NINE

BY THE TIME the Ross lands came into view, Glynis was sobbing and terrified. Caelan had not made a sound in over an hour. She'd been too scared to slow her progress and had not stopped to check on him. Now as men on horseback galloped toward them, she could not reel back her desperation.

"I cannot stop!" she yelled when Darach neared. "Caelan is unconscious."

"What happened?" Stuart jumped from his horse to take the reins from her bloodied hands. His darkened hazel gaze pinned her.

"Is he injured?" Darach asked, his voice booming.

"No, he has a fever. Became sick from exposure." She turned to look at Caelan over her shoulder. Jostling made it seem as if he moved, but it was the cart's wheels on the bumpy road.

Thankfully upon arriving, the brothers, joined by Artair carried Caelan into the house. Glynis remained by the cart barely noticing that stable lads came to retrieve the horses.

"We have to bandage yer hands." It was Grace, one of the kitchen maids who'd come to speak to her. She imagined her aunt and Cait were seeing about Caelan.

Glynis shook her head. "Please go help him. I can take care of my hands." The woman nodded and hurried off.

Instead of going to the house, Glynis went to the well, wincing as she pulled water from it. Then she carried the bucket to the side of the house where clothes were washed and poured water into a basin. It was soothing to dunk her hands into the cold water. Holding the reins for so many hours had caused blisters that had ruptured and bled.

"I'll wrap yer hands, lass," Lyall Ross, Caelan's uncle, said holding up strips of cloth.

"There is no need." Glynis held out her hand. "I can do it myself. Everyone should be concentrating on Caelan."

He ignored her and began to wrap the cloth around her hand. "The healer has been sent for. My nephew will recover. He always does."

"Is he prone to fevers?" Glynis asked looking past him to the house.

"Aye, he is. Since a lad, he's never done well with wet weather. I believe he was sick not that long ago. The rain and cold affected him this time."

Too weary to argue, she lifted the other hand, when he finished with the first. "Thank ye."

"Go see about food and rest. Ye will feel better after."

The words almost made her laugh. Glynis shook her head. "How can I feel better after everything I've done? Caelan is sick because of me." When a sob stuck in her throat, she gulped back it. "I am nothing but trouble."

"Get in the house," her aunt appeared in the doorway. "Ye must bathe and change clothes before ye too get sick."

Glynis threw herself to the floor and wrapped her arms around her aunt's legs. "I am so very sorry. Please forgive me."

Her aunt tugged at her until she stood. "Glynis, I understand ye and what ye've been through. I've told ye to stop and think before doing something. Ye are much too impulsive."

"And now Caelan is very ill because of me." She sobbed covering her face with both hands.

Her aunt took her hands from her face. He is awake and asking for food. Being out in the weather must have helped break the fever."

"Food?" Glynis sniffed loudly. "I will make a hearty soup for him."

"Ye will do no such thing," Maisie said. "I am boiling water for a warm bath for both ye and Mister Caelan. Now go on, miss. Go to yer bedchamber to wait."

The woman pushed a cup of something hot into her hands and gave her a gentle push toward the door. Unsure if there was something else she should do, Glynis peered over her shoulder to her aunt, who'd begun stirring a pot.

After bathing and having her hands salved and wrapped, Glynis fell into a deep sleep. She woke to find it was dark outside. Her stomach growled in hunger and she slid from the bed.

The moon gave enough light that with the help of the candle she carried, Glynis could see clearly. Not wishing to start a fire, she ate leftover cold meat with a slice of bread. Cool ale completed her simple meal and then she walked back out of the kitchen.

Caelan's room was just a door down, she needed to check to ensure he was indeed recovered. Her aunt could've said he was to ease her conscience.

Not wishing to alarm him, she turned the knob and opened the door slowly. Caelan was asleep. Head lolled to the side, his face was soft and his lips slightly parted. A soft snore sounded as she tiptoed in.

From the lack of a wet sheen on his brow and his flushed cheeks, it was evident he no longer had a fever. Instead, he breathed normally, his chest lifting and lowering with each breath.

Glynis studied him for a long moment, pictures of the night before forming. Her cheeks burned at the thought of what they'd done. She'd never be the same again, she was sure of it.

Another thing she was sure of was that never would she find another lover who would make her feel like Caelan.

"Goodness," she whispered and hurried from the room.

TWO DAYS LATER, the routine of men on patrol and seeing about their meals kept them very busy. Her aunt remained perturbed with her and Glynis did not blame her.

The third morning came along with it a light drizzle. Glynis trudged to the dining room and was astounded to see everyone already eating.

"I am glad ye got plenty of rest," Cait called out with a bright smile. "Come sit next to me. We must discuss plans to go to the village. Hopefully, the weather will get better."

"Ye should not be going anywhere," Stuart said with a frown. "What if something happens while ye are on the road."

Aunt Mariel huffed. "We will be riding in the carriage. It will be safe."

Noting that Caelan was not at the table, Glynis wondered if he remained abed. "Where is Caelan?" she whispered to Cait.

"In his bedchamber," she replied in an equally low tone.

"Lady Mariel will not allow him out of bed yet."

"He wishes to speak to ye," her aunt said, obviously eavesdropping on their conversation. "Go see him as soon as ye finish yer meal."

Despite being hungry, the food lost its luster. What would Caelan say to her? Would he blame her for being ill? It was without a doubt her fault, and she would apologize profusely.

"Aunt Mariel, I wish to discuss returning to Barra. I have been a horrendous guest. It is best I return home."

When Darach gave her a pointed look, it was discomfiting. "I suggest ye speak to Caelan first." He held her gaze long enough for her to realize he knew of what happened between them at the cottage.

Immediately her throat went dry, and a burning heat traveled from her neck up to her face. Thankfully, the cook walked in to place a platter of meat in the center of the table taking everyone's attention.

Everyone focused on the food except for Darach who looked at her again.

"I think I should go see about Caelan," Glynis whispered and pushed back from the table.

Her aunt gave her a quizzical look. "Ye should eat, dear."

"I will. In a few moments. I cannot rest until I apologize to him." Before anyone could stop her, Glynis hurried out of the room and down the side corridor to where Caelan was.

"Enter," he said, after she knocked twice. When she pushed the door open, she found Caelan sitting up in bed with a ledger on his lap. He looked up and his brows rose.

"Good morning, Glynis."

"Ye looked flushed, perhaps ye should not be working on

accounts, but instead resting," Glynis said not moving from the door.

With a shrug, he closed the ledger and placed it on the table beside the bed. "Stepmother insists on the raging fire in the hearth and the curtains drawn to keep the warmth in. It is suffocatingly hot in here."

The room was indeed hot. Glynis went to a window and pulled the curtain open. Immediately the room became lighter. "I will close it before I leave."

He cocked his head to the side. "Always rebellious."

Emboldened by his playful mood, she went to the bed and sat on the edge. "I must apologize to ye. I am so very sorry to have caused ye to be sick."

"It seems I have a weak constitution. I do not think to have fully recovered from being sick from a fortnight ago. I have tried to convince my stepmother that the cold is better for me than this heat. But after what happened, she will never believe me."

Glynis met his gaze, doing her best to push the pictures of him bereft of clothing from her mind. "Nonetheless, I caused this. For ye to be in bed recovering. Say ye will forgive me."

"We must speak about what happened at the cottage. That is more important than this constant need of yers to apologize. There could be repercussions for our actions. I take full responsibility."

Glynis bit her bottom lip. He sounded so English in the way he spoke that for a moment, she wished he continue. His accent was so soothing and soft.

"If ye are referring to the intimacy. There is no need to feel responsible. Our passions overtook our senses. In the both of us."

"Glynis," Caelan said in a firm tone. "What if ye are with child?"

She waved her hand dismissively. "Ye have to do something specific for that to happen. I am sure ye did not."

"I am very sure, I did," Caelan replied with a slight lift to the corners of his lips. "Ye are aware that when a man spills his seed it is what can cause the forming of a bairn. Are ye not?"

Her eyes rounded of their own volition. "Ye did that? Oh, goodness. I had no idea." She got to her feet. "I am sure that is not true."

"What specifically did ye think a man does to produce a child?"

Mind awhirl, she tried to remember what the young man she'd lost her virginity to had said. He'd said it would not happen because he held back. A maid had once told her, she had to remain on her back, legs up in the air to become with child. Another had said it only happened when a man loved the woman.

"Ye do not love me. Therefore, it will not happen. And I did not remain on my back with my legs…" She stopped speaking when he fought not to laugh out loud.

"This is not funny," Glynis snapped. "Ye are trying to scare me. To teach me a lesson."

"I am not," Caelan said. "We will marry swiftly. It is best. I will speak to my stepmother about it."

Glynis leaned forward and glared at him. "I am going home to Barra. I will not accept a marriage out of duty. When I marry it will be to someone who loves me, and I love." She stalked to the door only to gasp when Caelan took her arm and whirled her around.

He'd gotten from the bed so quickly that it was astonishingly clear he felt much better. His blue gaze was dark with annoyance. "I will not father a bastard. Ye and I will marry and that is all there is to it."

"Ye wish I had never come here. Admit it." Glynis looked into his eyes needing to hear the truth.

"Aye, I do," Caelan admitted. "At times, I do. However, we cannot change what has happened."

Despite admiring his honesty, her heart sank. She was a walking disaster.

CHAPTER TEN

"I TAKE IT yer talk did not go well." Darach stood at the doorway through which Glynis had just left.

"She is confused. I am sure things will work out," Caelan said, despite the fact he wasn't at all sure what the unpredictable woman would do next.

His brother chuckled. "Ye have no idea, do ye? I can say that if ye marry, it will be interesting to see what she does from one day to the next."

"Aye, I have no idea where she is at the moment or what she is doing. I have never known a more perplexing woman."

"Cait and mother are taking her to visit Bree in town."

Darach went to the window and pushed it open. "Why is it so hot in here?" He turned to the hearth and shook his head. "Mother."

"She will be cross seeing the window open." Caelan inhaled deeply. "It feels good to breathe fresh air."

His brother paced in thought. "I leave for the keep tomorrow. Perhaps it is best for ye, mother, and Glynis to return with me. There is much to be done. I am sure mother will wish to write the MacNeil's so they can travel for the wedding."

"Aye," Caelan said getting up from the chair he sat upon and going to the window. "This is not at all what I planned."

When Darach chuckled, Caelan narrowed his eyes. "Ye are

enjoying this, aren't ye?"

"Aye," Darach acknowledged. "Of all of us, I was sure ye would not marry unless it was well planned out. That my sweet cousin seduced the infallible Caelan Ross is… well, it's very entertaining."

"Glad that I can be of service to ye, Laird." Caelan motioned to the door. "I am in dire need of tea."

Thankfully the women were already outside and climbing into the carriage that would take them to the village, so his stepmother could not fuss over him being out of his bedchamber.

"Mister Caelan," Grace said as she hurried over to him. "Yer stepmother insisted ye remain abed today. I am to ensure it."

He walked past the well-meaning woman to the wooden box he kept loose tea in. "I will not tell if ye don't."

In the dining room, Stuart, Artair, and Darach studied a revised map of the surrounding lands. A man, who he assumed was the local mapmaker spoke in low tones while sketching on the large parchment.

Stuart met Caelan's gaze and then looked to the map. "I do believe the threat is gone for now. However, Cairn is out there, and we must find him."

"He will take time to lick his wounds, and it will take time for him to make another plan. However, we cannot let our guard down," Artair said staring down at the map.

"Just when I think we can rest easy, another threat raises its ugly head," Darach said with a sigh. "We must ensure the guards are extra vigilant."

Artair scratched his bearded chin. "I will ride with a pair of men to each outpost and speak to the men personally. Although I am sure we have good guards, it is easy to become complacent over time."

"That is a good idea," Darach said. "Go to the northern regions. Gideon visits his lands often, but I am not so sure it is to ensure safety, but more to get away from a persistent woman."

Caelan chuckled. "Is the widow still in pursuit?"

"Aye," Darach replied. "I will have to intervene soon. There is something about her I do not trust."

"Be with care, Artair," Stuart said. "Especially in the area directly north. There has been very little interaction between us and them. The village there is of a good size. I fear it would be easy for someone to blend in."

"How is yer leg?" Caelan asked.

Their cousin shrugged. "Better."

"Anton should return today or tomorrow at the latest. Let us wait to see what he has to report."

As if summoned, there were voices as someone came through the back kitchen door. Anton entered, looking weary.

"Just when I was about to give up and return. I saw him. He was speaking to two men just outside the village. They mounted and headed further south to the shoreline." Anton paused for breath. "I tried to beat them there to alert guards to stop them. But they could not find them."

Every one of their faces turned to stone. The man had escaped once again.

"I HAVE AN idea," Darach said. "But I must get back to the keep. I will speak to mother and convince her it is time to return," Darach continued, looking directly at Caelan. "After all, there is a wedding to prepare for."

His brothers and cousin all looked to him and Caelan's chest squeezed. "I am not sure how I feel about it."

Stuart cleared his throat. "Ye do not have to marry her if ye are not sure. It would be a great mistake."

"If she is with child, I will never allow for any bairn of mine to be born a bastard," he replied meaning it.

Darach nodded. "I understand. She is family. I think it is best ye marry the lass either way."

"I plan to," Caelan said. "In the meantime. I suppose we should return and wait."

THE VILLAGE WAS picturesque, and Glynis immediately fell in love. It wasn't so different from the villages on Barra, but here the people were warm and welcoming. As they walked through the newly built market, she could not believe the abundance of seafood and other items the merchants sold.

"Where do all these people come from?" she asked breathlessly as she and Cait managed to get through a crowd of women sifting through linens at a well-stocked stall.

"From the surrounding areas to the north and south. Since a horrible constable was sent away, people feel free to come here. Ye would be astounded if ye saw the difference from when we first arrived." Cait smiled widely when a child rushed to hand her a beautifully crafted clay pot. "From me mum for ye," the lad said then raced away.

"Goodness," Cait said looking across to nod at a woman

who waved back.

"That is the sweetest thing I have ever seen," Glynis exclaimed. "I would love to live here."

It was true, she could see herself living there. Of course, Cait and Stuart would have to extend the invitation.

"Ye are welcome to remain here with us as long as ye wish. It would be lovely," Cait said.

Glynis hoped with all her heart that Cait was sincere in her invitation and not just being polite. She'd wait and ask again when they returned to the house. If Stuart and Cait did not mind her staying, she would.

"I do believe the meal should be ready," Bree Ross said. "I told the cook to ensure to have my meat pies baked by now."

Bree and Dougal's house was near the village and within walking distance. However, with all their purchases, they had to climb back into the carriage to travel there.

Letting out a long sigh, Glynis peered at the passing scenery. "It is so very peaceful here."

"Now ye see why I love visiting Cait and Stuart," her aunt said with a soft smile.

Glynis nodded. "It is a beautiful place."

"I told Glynis she is welcome to remain here," Cait said brightly. "I do mean it." She met Glynis' gaze. "Ye can decide."

Her aunt gave her a warm look. "If it is what ye wish Glynis, I have no objection. It would be good for Cait to have company, especially with a bairn on the way."

Her aunt shrugged. "Of course, ye will have to send a message to yer parents about it."

"I would love nothing more," Glynis exclaimed with a wide smile. Meeting Cait's soft gaze she said, "Thank ye."

"Cait could use the company," Bree said. "Soon she will not be able to come to the village or leave the house."

"It is settled then," Cait said. "Ye will stay with us after Lady Mariel leaves."

Her aunt chuckled. "I may return with Darach. I must see about Beatrice and Isobel. So many grandchildren, I will be busy ensuring they all get to know me well."

"I am so happy for ye," Bree said with shiny eyes. "It is a wonderful life to spend with yer grandchildren, who will grow to love ye abundantly." She shook her head. "I can only pray that my sons marry and move closer so that I too can enjoy my grandchildren."

"After a while, I will ask for money from my family so that I can purchase land and build my own cottage," Glynis said. "I would love to be independent."

"What are ye saying child," her aunt said laughing. "Ye will be married and surrounded by bairns. I just know it. I am convinced Caelan just may be the man."

Her eyes widened. Was it noticeable that she and he had been intimate? What if what he said was right and she was already with child? "I am sure he is not."

Everyone giggled.

Bree placed her hand over Glynis' hand. "Tell us how he reacted upon finding ye in the cottage."

"He was furious and threatened to kick down the door. When he entered, he was sopping wet, and I felt horrible. Well, I was actually a bit scared of him, but other than a glare he went directly to the fireplace and undressed. Right there in front of me."

Everyone gasped and covered their mouths with both

hands, except for aunt who shook her head. "Men are so unabashed."

"What did ye do?" Cait asked, her eyes wide.

Glynis was enjoying telling the story. "I grabbed my cloak and threw it at him."

The laughter surrounded her, and she had to admit it was comical. "He looked ridiculous wrapped in my cloak while chastising me about my impulsiveness."

"I wish I could have seen it," Cait said wiping tears from the corners of her eyes.

Letting out a sigh, Glynis shook her head. "He was right of course. And because of it, he got very sick."

"He is fine now," her aunt said. "Caelan has always been that way since a wee lad. Got horribly sick one day and night and then recovers quickly."

Bree met her eyes. "Ye and he did not fight all night did ye?"

As the heat rushed from her chest to her face, Glynis looked down at her clutched hands. "No, we did not."

"Oh," Cait said and burst out laughing. "Ye kissed. Ye kissed," she repeated.

Bree bit her bottom lip in glee. "Is he a good kisser?"

"I am not speaking about it," Glynis said her face on fire.

"Tell us," Cait insisted. "He is so very charming, but a bit aloof. I cannot imagine him naked, wrapped in a cloak, kissing."

"Leave her be," her aunt said although she gave Glynis a questioning look. She too wanted to know what happened.

"Very well," Glynis said. "Aye, we kissed. And yes, he is a very good kisser. That is all I am willing to say on the matter."

While having a delicious meal at Bree's home and enjoying the entertainment of two boys she and her husband had adopted, Glynis became more convinced of wishing to live there.

Admittedly, what her aunt had said rang true. She did eventually wish for a family, one like Bree's away from the busyness of a keep, with only her family in the household.

"Where does Caelan live?" she asked Cait when they walked out to see Bree's garden.

"He shares a large home with Duncan and Beatrice. It is a beautiful house. However, it is away from the shoreline, which is on purpose as Duncan prefers to be away from views of the sea."

It was interesting to her that Caelan lived with Duncan and not closer to his mother's family. But it was something that Cait probably would not know the answer to. Instead, she inhaled a deep breath of salty air and looked down from the hill where the house sat. Below, the view of the village with all its people bustling here and there, preparing for the last needs of the day, made her smile. Past the village, the wide expanse of sea spread as far as the eye could see.

"Can I have a moment with Glynis?" her aunt asked, walking up to them.

"Aye, of course," Cait replied with a warm smile at Glynis. She'd never met someone so kind and warm. Glynis couldn't help but smile back.

"What is it, Aunt Mariel?" Glynis asked wrapping an arm around her waist. "Are ye going to try to convince me to return with ye?"

Her aunt met her gaze for a long moment and Glynis knew

whatever she was going to say was serious. "What exactly happened between ye and Caelan?"

The bottom dropped from her stomach, and her breath caught. "Nothing. We kissed that is all."

"When he asked to speak to ye this morning, I could tell something weighed heavy on his mind. I thought perhaps he wanted to chastise ye again. But now I think there is something more."

"No, not at all. That was it. He is still angry with me for running away. He thinks me childish and I do not blame him one bit."

Her aunt sighed. "Ye have never been a good liar, Glynis. If more happened between ye, I know Caelan and he will want to take responsibility."

"I cannot marry him," Glynis replied. "I will not hold him responsible for something that both of us did of our own free will. It is not fair."

"What of the consequences?" her aunt asked.

"There will not be any. I am sure of it," Glynis said and immediately recalled her conversation with Caelan. He'd said he had spilled his seed and it could bring forth a bairn. She pushed it from her mind. "I wish to remain here. Start a life away from all the memories and not be a bother to anyone."

"Unfortunately, that is not to be for now. Ye will return to the keep and we will wait to see if ye are indeed with child. If ye are, ye will marry Caelan. He will never allow a child of his to grow up fatherless. My husband gave him the Ross last name but never let him forget the circumstance of his birth."

Glynis squeezed her eyes shut. "I shouldn't have allowed it to happen. But it was wonderful, Aunt Mariel. So very wonderful."

Her aunt chuckled. "I am not sure ye should be sharing this with me about my own stepson."

"I have to tell someone," Glynis said. "I have never thought such wonder could happen between a man and a woman. I yearn for it to happen again. But I know it should not."

"It certainly should not," her aunt said sternly. "Ye and Caelan must remain apart until we know if ye are with child."

"So, we will return to the keep?" she asked allowing her gaze to travel across the view again. "Or can we remain here and wait?"

Her aunt studied her for a moment and then she too looked to the sea. "We can wait here. When do yer monthly courses usually come?"

"Any day now actually," Glynis said. "Ye will see that nothing came of it." It was convincing to state the words, and in her mind, Glynis was sure nothing would come of what had transpired between her and Caelan.

The only thing was, that each time she thought of them alone in the cottage, both fully naked and entwined with one another, her body screamed for him. Just picturing Caelan that night, face taut as he made love to her, made it difficult to concentrate or think clearly.

"Oh no," her aunt said cutting through her musing. "I have a feeling it is best for Caelan to go. Ye and he cannot be allowed any opportunity for what happened to be repeated."

IT WAS LATE by the time they returned to the house. Darach announced that he and his men would be returning the next day and that both Glynis and her aunt should pack to go with them.

“I will certainly not be prepared to go tomorrow,” her aunt said giving her son a pointed look.

“Mother, we should speak,” Darach replied, guiding her to Stuart’s study.

“Come Caelan,” her aunt called over her shoulder.

Glynis waited to see if they would call her, but they did not. She huffed in annoyance, especially when Caelan glanced in her direction before following his stepmother and brother.

“I hope he will not insist on ye leaving,” Cait said slipping her arm through Glynis’. Come let us have some peppermint tea and relax.” They walked to the kitchen where Clara and the two cooks already sat talking.

The atmosphere in the kitchen instantly relaxed Glynis. Truth be told, she was certain her aunt would stand her ground, so there was no need to worry.

CHAPTER ELEVEN

"IT MAKES LITTLE sense for ye and Glynis to remain here," Caelan argued. "She left once without notice and can do so again at any time."

"I doubt it will come to that," his stepmother replied. "She's learned her lesson about consequences."

Darach shrugged. "If she is not with child and wishes to remain here, what then?"

"I will write a letter to my brother and ask that he send the necessary support for her to remain. All they wish is the best for her. After the horrendous attack on her and Gavin, I cannot imagine how she feels."

"If ye are certain Mother, then I leave the decision up to Caelan as to whether ye go or remain."

His stepmother spoke up immediately, not allowing him an opportunity. "Caelan, ye must go. As soon as I find out either way, I will send a message. I do not trust ye both under the same roof right now."

"What?" Caelan narrowed his eyes. "What did Glynis say to ye?"

His stepmother pressed her lips together. "I will only say that the way the lass shared what occurred made it obvious she would not hesitate to repeat the experience."

Darach threw his head back and laughed. "Good on ye,

brother."

When Lady Mariel gave him a stern look Darach fought to keep from chuckling, failing miserably.

"Ye should go as planned, Caelan," Lady Mariel continued. "I will remain here and keep a keen eye on Glynis. She is sure there is naught to fret about."

"She also thought one had to be in love to produce a bairn," Caelan couldn't help interjecting. "Do not trust her word."

THAT NIGHT WHILE sleeping, Caelan became aware someone had entered his bedroom. Years of being a trained warrior meant he was always prepared. However this night, Caelan wasn't sure if it were a real person or a dream.

"Caelan."

"Caelan."

"Are ye awake?"

The whispers permeated through the fog of sleep until he realized indeed someone was in his bedchamber. Caelan sat straight up bumping his forehead into another.

"Ouch!" Came the whispered exclamation that echoed what he'd thought at the same time.

"Glynis. What are ye doing? Why are ye here?"

The lass pushed his leg away and plopped onto the bed. "I was thinking. If I were with bairn—which I am not—I still wish to remain here."

Caelan rubbed his eyes, unable to see in the dark more than her outline. "Glynis, it is not up for discussion. We will marry, and ye will come to live with me in my house. I am responsible for the clan ledgers and therefore must remain close to Darach."

"Ye do not have to live here with me," she hissed. "I am informing ye that I will remain here. Ye are not in love with me, therefore it makes little sense for us to live together.

"I want to be a father who is present in my children's lives."

"Ye can visit every sennight…or two."

"If I am married, I wish to have all the privileges that come with it."

"We can be together every sennight."

"And if ye become with child more than once, ye will still insist on living apart?"

He couldn't help enjoying the banter with the annoyingly unpredictable lass.

"I suppose over time, as we grow old, we will wish to live together then. I mean by then we may be in love."

"Glynis."

"Caelan."

"No."

"No, what?"

"No, I will not allow my wife to live over a day's ride away from me."

"Then if for some reason we have to marry, ye will move here."

Instead of a response, Caelan grabbed her and pulled her to lay on the bed. He was nude as he'd already packed most his clothing, leaving out only what he would wear the next day.

"Why are ye always naked?"

He took her mouth, and immediately fire burned through every inch of his being. The wench would not leave his bed, not for a long while.

The thin fabric of her chemise made it easy to do away with. Caelan took to her breasts, first one, then the other as she clawed at his back and arched up, lifting up to touch her sex to his.

Sliding his hand down her side, he held her hips steady and rubbed his thick hard staff through the folds of her sex.

Immediately he had to cover her mouth as she cried out his name. "Shhh," he commanded, covering her mouth while continuing to move his hips causing a friction that threatened to undo him.

"I cannot take ye fully," he whispered in her ear while sliding his finger into her, teasing the nub between her folds with his thumb. "I wish I could. Ye feel so wet and inviting."

Glynis moaned pulling his face down to hers and kissing him with inexperienced but enticing passion.

Placing himself over her, once again he slid up and down, his staff so hard he could barely breathe.

When she clawed at his bottom, urging him forward, he was unable to deny her. Caelan lost to the pull of want, adjusted, and plunged into her hot wetness. Both gasped at the wonderful feeling that exploded around them.

"Ah!" Caelan exclaimed when he began moving faster and harder. He drove in fully before pulling out and thrusting again.

When she shuddered in completion, he felt his entire body tighten with the threat of his own desire overcoming him, and using all the willpower he could muster, Caelan withdrew and spilled onto the bedding.

"Oh, no," Glynis whispered. "Did ye do that thing again?"

Caelan could barely breathe, as waves of the aftermath worked through him.

"What?" He collapsed over her, unable to move, his body plaint.

"The thing that could cause bairns."

"No." He wasn't in the state to explain to her. Instead, he covered her mouth with his, taking all she had left to give.

When he woke the following morning, the bed was empty. However, her scent remained. All over him.

"GOOD MORNING," HIS aunt said in greeting when he walked into the kitchen. "Ye are the last one to rise. Darach was about to send someone to wake ye."

"Where is he?"

"Outside. He and Stuart are having one last walk about before ye leave." His stepmother poured hot water into a cup and placed a twisted bundle of tea leaves in cheesecloth into it. "I wish ye would have brought more," she told him.

"I will ask Artair to check with the merchant ships when he travels north. There could be some that carry black tea," he drank the dark bitter beverage.

While buttering his bread, he peered to the dining room. "Where is Glynis?"

"She went to her bedchamber after breaking her fast. Seemed a bit somber this morning. Ye should speak to her before leaving. Ensure the lass all will be well. She needs to hear it from ye."

Caelan let out a breath avoiding his stepmother's gaze. "I

will."

After eating, he went to gather his trunk and scabbard. He loaded the items onto a wagon and then went to the stables to find his horse.

The steed pawed at the dirt, seeming to know they were to travel. Caelan rubbed his hand down the animal's nose. "We are about to go home."

"I will saddle him, Mister Caelan. Is there anything else ye need?" a lanky man asked approaching.

"Ensure he eats his fill of oats and has plenty of water," Caelan replied.

Once he was assured his instructions would be followed, he turned toward the house. Glynis stood outside the kitchen door looking toward him.

When he approached her face pinkened. "Good morning," she murmured. "Ye are leaving?"

"Aye. It is best that I do since we cannot seem to keep from one another."

She leaned forward. "I wished to talk. Not for what happened to happen."

"Ye seemed to want it when it was happening."

"Be that as it may, we did not come to an understanding." She glanced around to ensure no one heard. "And aye, it was very nice."

"Nice," he cocked a brow. "Glynis, we will wait to find out whether ye are with child or not. If ye are, we will marry immediately. If ye are not…" He took her hand and lifted it to his lips. "I still insist on marrying. However, we can wait until a time when both yer family and mine can be in attendance."

Her eyes widened and she pulled her hand away from his,

albeit slowly. "Ye, insist we marry?"

"Aye, I do."

"Oh." She frowned and bit her bottom lip. "I suppose I am not opposed. However, I insist that I will live here."

Caelan closed his eyes and slowly blew out a breath. "No."

"I like it here."

"Ye can visit."

"Or ye can visit me."

"Stop being so stubborn."

"Am I the one who is unbending?"

"I would describe ye as the one being more selfish."

"I am not." Glynis glared up at him.

"Ensure to let me know as soon as ye are sure. Either way." He leaned forward and planted a kiss on her parted lips. "I await the message."

With that, he turned away and walked into the kitchen to bid his stepmother and Cait farewell.

THE RIDE BACK to Keep Ross went fast. Probably because the entire time Caelan thought about Glynis and hating that he'd not see her every day. Was it that he had fallen in love with the willful lass? The last thing he needed in his life was disorder and Glynis was not someone who would ever conform.

He had the feeling no matter what he decided or stated, she'd always argue the point. His lips curved at her odd acceptance of his marriage proposal. Only she could affect him in such a way that he'd proposed most informally.

"I suppose I am not opposed." He chuckled at remembering her reply.

"Caelan!" Artair called out while guiding his large warhorse toward him. "Did ye see that?"

He hated admitting to having his head in the clouds but when it came to danger, he was not about to lie. "I was not paying attention. What is it?"

"I thought I heard voices."

He and Artair had gone ahead of the others as scouts. Admittedly, it was probably the wrong job for him at the moment.

"Aye, I can hear them," he said looking toward the woods. "Women."

They guided the horses slowly in the direction of the voices, stopping when able to see a flowing creek.

On the shore and in the shallow water, a trio of women were bathing. Not too far away, several men and a few bairns were in a camp they had set up.

"Travelers," Artair said. "Should be harmless."

His cousin studied him as they rode back to the road. "What has ye so distracted?"

"I cannot help but wonder if I am making a mistake with Glynis," he replied.

Artair shook his head. "Other than being a monk, sooner or later something like this will happen. Ye will marry the lass. She is a good match for ye."

"Why do ye believe that?"

"I have always felt that ye require a strong Highland woman to keep ye from yerself."

Caelan gave him a bland look. "Whoever I marry will not change me."

"Ha!" Artair let out a bark of laughter. "She already has. We just rode past the road that leads to our home."

As they turned the horses around to gallop back to inform the rest there were no threats, Artair kept laughing making Caelan want to pull his sword and smack him on the back of the head.

CHAPTER TWELVE

GLYNIS HURRIED FROM the kitchen behind Maisie with a pot of oats and a ladle. They served the men who filled every one of the four tables in the dining room.

Helping with the daily tasks of cooking, serving, and washing of tunics made the days pass quickly.

When she walked into the front room later that morning, her aunt sat in a chair with embroidery on her lap. In another chair, Clara knitted, while Cait and her companion, Cora, could be seen through the window walking.

"It is a good day," Glynis said sitting down and letting out a breath. "I like life here. I feel useful."

Her aunt tore her gaze from the window and looked at her. "That is because Darach has sent twenty men to guard us. Normally, we would not be so busy."

"They have little to do, other than patrol," Clara said.

Just then, Lyall Ross walked into the room. "Ladies." His gaze went directly to Clara, who blushed and avoided looking at him.

Glynis couldn't help but smile. "Mister Ross."

"There is a message from the laird for ye," he handed it to her aunt. Then glancing toward Cait's mother once more, he turned and walked out.

"Why do ye not admit to the feelings ye have?" her aunt

teased. "A second chance at love is wonderful Clara."

The woman nodded. "It is so strange. I am not sure how to handle it."

"Who sends the message?" Glynis asked, wondering if it was from her family.

Her aunt looked to the paper in her hand and unfolded it. She skimmed the words before looking to her. "Caelan grows impatient for news."

"I-I am not sure what to think," Glynis said biting her lip. "How long has it been since they left. Only a few days."

Her aunt gave her a knowing look. "It has been two weeks. We must prepare to travel back to Keep Ross." She stood and hurried out of the room, with Glynis on her heels. "Where are ye going?"

"I must reply to Caelan and send a messenger to yer parents."

"About what?" Glynis said her heart racing. "A few more days. I am sure…"

Her aunt blew out a breath. "I should have acted sooner. It is apparent ye are with child."

"No." It was all she could say, as it occurred to her that indeed, her monthly flow had not come yet. With all the busy work of taking care of guardsmen, she'd not had time to think about it.

"I will pack," she told her aunt, not wanting to cause more concern.

Her aunt smiled. "I need to return to see about the new bairn. Although her mother is with her, I wish to see Beatrice."

As Glynis walked to her bedchamber, she considered how many Ross children there were. Ewan and Catriona had three,

Darach and Isobel one. Soon Beatrice and Cait would deliver another pair.

She placed her hand over her stomach. If she was indeed with child, she would give birth to the seventh Ross child. Her breath caught at considering her parents' reaction to the news that she was to marry Caelan Ross.

Would they be angry? Furious? She paced the small bedchamber. Although bastard born, Caelan had the Ross last name. He had land and in all probability plenty of coin.

Her parents had never expressed wanting to match her or her brothers with anyone, instead insisted they be intelligent in their choice of who they marry. Her older brother had married a woman who was from a well-established family. Gavin would in all probability marry someone who saw past his disfigurement and still loved him. He had to marry; otherwise, Glynis would hate what happened to him even more.

Pushing away the guilt, she pulled dresses and other items from the wardrobe and began to pack.

FOR THE ENTIRE journey to Keep Ross, Glynis fretted. In a way, she did not wish to arrive. She'd yet to accept the fact of being with child and once there and facing Caelan, it would become real.

Admittedly, she'd not had monthly courses since arriving and was due to have them just after she and Caelan had been together.

In her mind, it was hard for the realization to sink in. A bairn. With someone she barely knew. All because of her impetuous nature.

There had been thoughts of asking her parents to take her

back home. To avoid seeing Caelan and leave him a note asking that he not follow. She'd gone so far as to write it out, just in case she could get her parents alone and tell them she would rather raise a child alone than to force a man to marry her. But in the end, she'd balled it up and thrown it into the fire.

Her father would refuse. Hopefully, he'd not attack Caelan at first sight for having dared to touch his daughter. Elliott MacNeil remained youthful and very agile. He practiced at swordfight at least twice weekly, keeping a rigid routine to ensure he remained in fighting shape.

Since the attack, he'd become even more strict when it came to training. It was not only she who desired revenge.

The keep came into view. She let out a long breath at spotting the tall gray walls that surrounded the imposing structure.

"We have arrived," her aunt said needlessly. "I am so glad to be home. I missed sleeping in my bed."

When Glynis did not reply, Lady Mariel covered her hand. "All will be well. Ye will see. Once ye are married and settled, ye will think on this day with fondness."

"What if he resents me for putting him in this situation?" Glynis asked, her gaze glued to the keep. "It would be a miserable life to be tied to someone that does not care for ye."

Her aunt huffed. "Glynis, both of ye took part in the situation, as ye put it. How can he place blame solely on ye?"

"It was because I ran off. My doing it was what brought this to happen." Her stomach churned. She was going to be sick. "Pl-please stop the carriage."

The carriage barely stopped when she got out and lost all the contents of her stomach. Everything seemed to spin, and she squeezed her eyes shut. "I do not feel well at all."

"Oh, dear. I was wondering if ye were going to be one of the lucky few who do not get ill."

Glynis moaned and got sick again. Thankfully, she was able to rinse her mouth out and within a few minutes was well enough to ride again.

By the time they rode through the gates however, she was too unwell to get up from the seat.

"Please call Caelan to come at once. Glynis requires assistance." Her aunt spoke to someone and moments later, she was carried from the carriage and into a bedchamber.

Glynis was too dizzy to keep track of who undressed her and slipped a nightshirt over her head. She was settled into a bed, with pillows behind her back, as lying flat made her sick.

"I feel horrible," she said when a young maid neared with a bowl of clear broth. "I cannot possibly drink it."

"Ye must put something into yer stomach," Isobel Ross, the laird's wife entered. "Try at least some of the toasted bread."

Just the thought of food made her gag, but she pushed through and managed a couple of bites of bread. She waited a bit and drank from the bowl. Despite her stomach's protests, the contents stayed down.

"I did not plan to return and be nursed," Glynis told Isobel, who motioned to maids to take out the bucket she'd become ill into and clean it out.

She and Isobel had gotten to know one another when she, Darach, and her aunt had come to visit the MacNeil's in Barra.

"I got sick too. It is horrible." Isobel lowered to sit and took her hand. "Do not fret, it should not last long."

"Just a few days?" Glynis asked.

Isobel's expression tightened. "A few weeks."

Glynis moaned, covering her face with both hands. "I will die."

When Isobel laughed, Glynis wanted to glare at her.

"Ye will not die. I do know it is a most disagreeable feeling."

She looked from Isobel to the hearth, where a cheery fire burned, and then to the door.

"Where is Caelan?"

Isobel shrugged. "A messenger was sent to his house earlier. I am surprised he has not appeared yet."

"He may not wish to see me." Glynis tried to lift her arms to see about her hair, but every movement made the room sway. "Oh, no, I think I am about to be sick again."

Just as a maid hurried in, Isobel stood. "I will ask Greer to boil some herbs to help settle yer stomach."

Glynis held up a hand. "Nothing that could harm the bairn."

"Of course," Isobel said leaving.

The maid lingered, her curious gaze on Glynis.

"Ye may go," Glynis said feeling a bit ill at ease at the woman's curious scrutiny.

The maid shook her head. "Ladies Isobel and Mariel have asked that ye not be left alone."

"What is yer name?" Glynis asked, attempting to push the nausea aside.

"Jane," the maid replied. "Are ye to marry, Mister Caelan?"

"Why do ye ask?" Glynis studied Jane.

Jane moved to the window and blew out a breath. "I am

curious. It is certainly unexpected that Mister Caelan would marry." After a light one-shouldered shrug, she was silent.

Before she could ask the woman why she made the comment, Glynis' stomach turned and the small amount of broth she'd had made a second appearance.

When her aunt came to visit later that evening, Glynis was happy to see her. Finally, her stomach had settled, and she was ravenous.

A maid walked in with a tray that had watery soup with only bits of meat and some toasted bread.

"I am hungry. That will not do," Glynis protested.

Her aunt smiled. "Once ye try it, we will see if it stays down. After, ye can have a bit of something more substantial."

She ate the bread and some of the broth. "Please can I have whatever I smell that the others are having?"

Her aunt nodded and the maid smiled. "Aye, miss. I will return shortly."

"Who is she?" Glynis asked. "Can I have her as my personal maid?"

"Of course," her aunt replied. "She is newly hired. Her name is Agnes."

Unsure how to breach the subject, Glynis met her aunt's gaze. "Caelan is not coming, is he?"

"He and several guards are on patrol in the southeastern corner of the isle. I do not know for sure if those are his lands or Duncan's." Her aunt made a dismissive motion with her hand. "I suppose it doesn't matter. They are due to return in another day. He's not aware of our return."

"I see." Glynis frowned.

"Is something else the matter?" her aunt asked.

"The maid who was here earlier. The large bosomed one. She made a comment alluding to not thinking Caelan would ever marry. Why would she say that?"

"Whatever she said is not something ye should fret about. She has never hidden her desire to be with Caelan. We've always ignored it, but perhaps it is time for her to no longer serve here."

Glynis noted that her aunt had not seemed surprised at what the maid had said. "Are ye sending a missive to my parents?"

Her aunt nodded. "The messenger leaves in the morning. It was too late to send it by the time I settled and had time to breathe."

"How do ye think they will react? Father, will be very angry."

Her aunt nodded. "I cannot imagine him not reacting strongly. I'd hoped to speak to Caelan before they clashed. It is now in God's hands." Her aunt shook her head and smiled. "Fortunately there is a bairn, and yer father will forgive everything upon its birth."

"What if he wants nothing more to do with me?" Tears spilled down her cheeks. "I am so embarrassed."

"There is no need," her aunt said moving to the bed and holding her. "I will handle my brother. Do not fret."

CHAPTER THIRTEEN

THE DAY HAD gone completely awry Caelan considered as he fought men who seemed to have appeared out of nowhere.

He fought with all his might, but there were too many and then pain radiated through as he was struck on the back of the head.

When Caelan came to, he was sitting on the ground tied to a tree. His shirt had been removed and his back was throbbing. It was then he recalled what had caused him to pass out. He'd been whipped until losing consciousness.

He'd been on patrol with four guards and when they'd stopped in a village, they separated. He'd been ambushed while making his way to meet the guards at the tavern for a meal.

Never in his life had he felt so much pain as when being lashed by the man he vowed to kill.

How had Duncan withstood so many years of imprisonment and beatings?

"Water," he croaked, barely able to speak past his dry tongue and throat.

"The beauty awakes," a gruff voice announced.

His head was yanked back by the hair. He grimaced but opened his mouth to the ale that was being poured. Trying to drink as much as he could, he began to choke and coughed up some of the ale.

The men laughed and one slapped him hard across the face. His cheek stung from it and he tasted blood. He couldn't make out who did it. By the inability to see well, he gathered both of his eyes were swollen shut.

He did his best to pry his eyes open and they did, but barely enough to see who his captors were, but none of them were recognizable.

By the dimness of the area, it was late in the day. Someone had to be out looking for him by now.

"What do ye plan to do with me?"

His captors ignored him.

He tried to ask again, but instead gave in to the lull of unconsciousness.

WHEN CAELAN WOKE next, he realized he had been thrown into the back of a wagon. It was the type used to transport prisoners.

The ale must have been drugged because by the brightness of the sun, it was well into the next day.

He scrambled to stand doing his best to move past the excruciating pulls of the skin of his back and the thundering headache.

They were near the sea, possibly going to a ship that took prisoners to mainland Scotland to be tried.

How did these men think to get away with this? He was well known on South Uist and not only that, but he'd speak to the captain of the ship and explain to him exactly who he was. The ones who should go to prison were the ones who brought him there.

It could be they planned to drug him again. When the wagon slowed, Caelan fell back to the floor pretending to remain unconscious.

The light from the opening of the back door made him aware they planned to give him more of the drugged ale.

"He remains passed out," one of them said.

"We should wake him. Don't want 'im wakin' up while we give him over," the other said.

Straining to see if there was another man, he could not hear much over the sounds of the grunts of the men who rolled him to his back.

It took monumental effort to keep from howling at the pain it caused. One of the men slapped him, the other poured warm liquid over his face. They held his nose and mouth shut until he fought to breathe.

"Awake now are ye?" one said chuckling.

Together, they dragged him from the wagon and held him down. When they tried to pour the ale down his throat, he spit it at them, gagging up the rest as he did his best not to swallow.

"Open yer damned mouth," one said kicking him in the side.

"If we kill him, the man who paid us will never know," the one who sat on Caelan said. "We have our coin."

"I have coin, I can pay," Caelan managed to say. "Let me go."

One of the men peered down at him. "We do not have time to go with ye and get more. We already took what ye had in yer purse and it was a good sum."

Caelan almost cried with relief when the man finally got up

from him and the men dragged him into the forest.

"Let's tie 'im to the tree," one said. "Here." One of them handed something to the other. "Leave this here. They will blame Cairn for it."

Once they ensured he was bound well and could not get away, one leaned forward. "Ye want some of the ale? That way ye will not feel it as much."

"No," Caelan replied, looking the man straight in the eyes.

The men exchanged looks. Then one stuck his dagger into Caelan's chest. His eyes widened at the knowledge he would die that day. When the dagger pierced the second time, darkness fell.

Surprisingly, the stabs did not hurt as much as his back. While dragging him to the tree, the deep lash wounds had opened back up and now burned. The pain is what brought him back from unconsciousness.

He'd not died yet. But it would not be long. It was almost impossible to take a breath and he fought for each one.

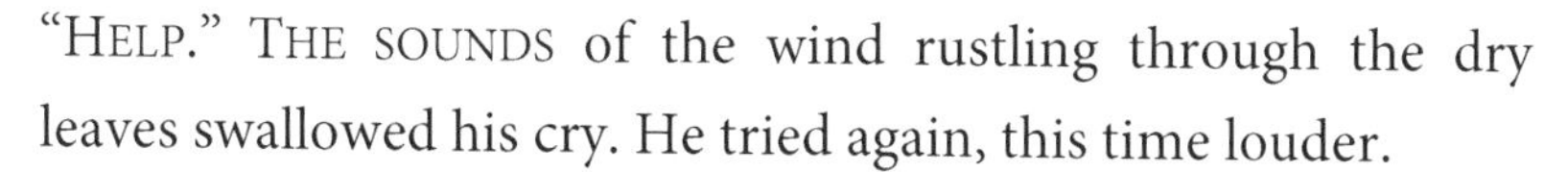

"HELP." THE SOUNDS of the wind rustling through the dry leaves swallowed his cry. He tried again, this time louder.

"Help me."

No one in their right mind would be out this late. It was almost sundown, and the weather was becoming colder, the wind piercing his fevered skin.

In the darkness of the forest, was how he'd meet his end? Caelan prayed to die quickly before a beast found him and decided to make a meal.

When tears trickled down his face, he could not stop the sobs of despair. This was not how he'd expected to die.

In battle, yes. From illness, perhaps. But not like this. Tied to a tree. Alone, cold, and in so much pain that he kept passing out.

If only he could take deep breaths, he could call out for help. But the stab must have penetrated his lungs, and he could not.

What would become of Glynis if she was indeed with child? His bairn would be born a bastard and although he was sure he or she would be welcomed by the Ross clan, the stigma of their birth would remain for their entire life.

He prayed for a girl. It would be much easier then.

When he tried to pull at the ropes, he groaned at the pain it caused. After many tries with little result, he could not fight any longer and once again passed out.

A MOAN WOKE him and Caelan was astonished to still be alive. He took shallow breaths and did his best to open his eyes, but they'd swollen further, and it proved impossible.

Despite his inability to move—as his body did not obey his commands to do so—he instinctively knew he was not tied to the tree any longer.

"Are ye awake young man?" The voice of an older man fell over him. "Ye are lucky to be alive. Thought ye were dead when I found ye."

"Leave him in peace," a woman said. "He may not live much longer."

"We should at least find out who he is," the man said. "Send word to his family."

"Escaped prisoner. Did ye not see the lash marks."

The man chuckled. "Ye are daft woman. Why would someone escape and tie themselves to a tree?"

Despite trying his best to speak, he could not make himself. The warmth of a tear trickling down his face was at least a sensation of remaining alive. The rest of his body however, seemed to have died.

Someone lifted his head. "Try to drink," the man's gravelly voice said. "I'd prefer ye to live. Ye seem highborn and perhaps yer family will pay for yer rescue."

The water soothed his parched throat, but it was bitter as if some sort of herbs had been added. He drank it all, not caring at this point what it was other than it was wet.

"They will most probably blame ye for what happened to him," the woman said chuckling. "People like him do not pay. Ye should have left 'im in the forest."

The man huffed. "Go away with ye. Ye are a useless old hag."

Caelan tried to talk, but his tongue was heavy and thick. When he tried to say Ross, it sounded more like a cough.

"Is he trying to talk?" the old woman asked, and someone poked him in the side. "Who are ye?"

"Leave 'im be," the man said. "He'll talk when he's ready."

A TRICKLE OF sunlight pierced past the discolored window curtain. Caelan wasn't sure how many days he'd been in the cottage. He'd become very ill, feverish for days, and at times prayed for death to claim him. The wounds on his back had begun to heal, but still every movement brought piercing pain.

At least he could see now, his eyes opening enough that he

made out the surroundings. He lay on a blanket on a dirt floor. Across from him were a cot, table, and two chairs.

The humble surroundings were tidier than he expected.

The old man had never told him his name, instead he'd fed Caelan and spent his days arguing with the woman who stopped by daily. Their odd friendship was entertaining. It was evident they found joy in the banter.

There was no one in the cottage. The old man usually spent his days fishing or foraging for berries and other plants to cook.

The door opened and the woman walked in. She glanced around the cottage and then to him.

"Ye seem better this morning. Can ye tell me who ye are?"

Despite the friendship that seemed to exist between her and his rescuer, Caelan wasn't sure he trusted her. He would wait for the man to come and hope he'd help him get word to his family.

"Where am I?" His voice sounded unfamiliar. Huskier.

"South Uist," the woman replied. "Are ye from 'ere?"

Caelan looked past her while attempting to get up. "Aye."

"Ye cannot leave. Rufus will be cross. I will go fetch him." The woman dashed from the cottage.

It took several tries for him to stand. Without shoes and tunic, only his torn breeches, he looked like a beggar.

The room swayed and he staggered to the table. There was nothing to eat in the cottage. The old man lived off the meager fish he caught, rarely having bread or anything else.

When the old man finally arrived much later, Caelan could barely remain awake. He was hungry and still too ill to stay upright, so he'd returned to the blanket to sleep.

"Young man," the old man prodded. "I caught several fish and was fortunate to have traded two for these." He held up some carrots. "The stew will be flavorful tonight."

With a wide grin, the old man hurried to the table to begin preparing the food.

Caelan looked at the man. "My name is Caelan Ross, I am brother to the laird."

CHAPTER FOURTEEN

"A GIRL," AUNT Mariel said with a wide smile. "Beatrice and Duncan will name her Gwendolyn. Which is beautiful, is it not?"

Glynis looked away from the blanket she was making. "It is a beautiful name."

"Yer parents should have arrived back at home by now."

"Hopefully, safely," Glynis replied.

Her mother and father had come to visit and to show their disapproval of what she'd done. However, with the fact that Caelan was gone and presumed dead, they were restrained in speaking ill of him. Deciding to not prolong their stay, they'd stayed for a sennight before returning home.

Although they'd asked her to return with them, it was obvious they preferred she did not. It would be easier for her to remain at Keep Ross and away from the gossips of her village in Barra.

"Midday meal is ready," Agnes, her maid, appeared at the sitting room doorway.

Glynis followed her aunt through the busy great room to the smaller dining room. The constant activity of the keep was a good distraction from the constant worry of what happened.

Every day, different groups of guards scoured the isle searching for Caelan. Men from Clan Macdonald and Clan

MacNeil had come to help, some of them returning to their homelands to search in case he was taken there.

Darach demanded that every village be searched and rewards for information were promised. So far, it had proved futile.

A group of warriors, including Stuart, Gideon, and Ewan had gone to find the man they thought responsible. The elusive, Cairn McInerny.

Although Glynis had never met the man, she hated him with all her being. He'd done what he'd set out to do. He'd brought Laird Ross and his brothers to their knees in despair and worry.

When entering the dining room, Glynis was surprised that Darach was there, as well as Angus Ross, the laird's uncle and Artair's father.

Isobel motioned for her to sit in the empty seat next to her.

The men ate in silence, acknowledging her with only a nod.

Since Caelan had been taken, Catriona, Ewan's wife, had returned to live at the keep. Cait was also brought to live there.

The women had been her support and comfort as the reality of her new life began to sink in. She was to be the mother to a fatherless bairn. It wasn't said—no one dare—but everyone suspected that Caelan had been killed and would never return.

For many days and nights, Glynis grieved him. The lost opportunity to being married to a man like him. The fact that he would never know their child and worse that his fear of fathering a bastard son would now come to be.

"Ye should eat," Isobel said bringing Glynis from her thoughts.

"Aye, I can finally eat without becoming ill," she replied and attempted to smile.

She considered there was much to do to prepare for the bairn. Fortunately, she had options about where to live and how to provide for the child. Darach had assumed responsibility for her and offered her a choice of whether to remain at Keep Ross or return with Stuart and Cait to their home.

Cait had insisted she return and live with them, which Glynis strongly considered. Beatrice and Duncan had invited her to live with them, since that was also Caelan's home.

"We will go visit Beatrice today," Isobel said. "Ye should come."

"I would love it."

THE RIDE TO the house where Duncan, Beatrice, and Caelan lived was a pair of hours, but it was a pleasant one as the surrounding scenery was filled with beautiful landscapes and a few farms and homes. Isobel, Agnes, and her aunt Mariel joined her in the carriage.

"Annis should be here already," Isobel said referring to her companion. "She and Orla are planning to help prepare our bedchambers for the stay."

The incredible lands surrounding the estate came into view. It was a beautiful house with stables, and several outhouses for guards and whoever worked there. To the left of the house was a large field and to the right behind the stables was what looked to be an area used for some sort of plantings. Currently, the ground was bare.

THEY ARRIVED AND were greeted by Beatrice's companion,

Orla. The young woman was beaming with happiness as she told them about the newly born babe.

Unable to keep from it, Isobel raced up the stairs to visit her sister. Wishing to give the sisters some time, Glynis remained in the main room.

"Would ye like to see the house?" Orla asked.

An overwhelming sadness enveloped her. She sensed Caelan in every place her gaze landed. "I would."

Orla motioned to the end of the hallway. This is where Mister Caelan spends a great deal of his time. The woman walked to a door and pushed it open.

Inside were bookcases, a desk, and two chairs. The room was dim as it had no window, yet it didn't seem gloomy.

Glynis walked in and went to the desk on which a stack of ledgers were set on one side and an open one in the center. Ensuring not to touch the quill stuck into an ink bottle, she ran her fingers over the neat rows of notes and numbers.

Caelan had exquisite penmanship. Of course, he did. Everything about him was orderly.

The books on the shelves were just as neat, each one set just right, the titles unknown to her for the most part.

Glynis closed her eyes and took in a breath as she tried to keep from weeping. "He is very orderly, is he not?" Her voice caught on the last word.

"He never allows us to clean this room. Prefers to do it himself. Says we might misplace something important." Orla laughed, making Glynis grateful the woman seemed to understand she needed distraction.

"What else is down this hall?" Glynis asked hurrying out of the study.

They walked into a beautiful parlor that once again seemed to exude Caelan's personality. From there, they went up the stairs, past Isobel and Duncan's bedchamber until reaching the end where it curved to the left.

Orla stopped and pointed to a door at the end of the short corridor. "That is his bedchamber."

When the young woman remained standing, Glynis understood this was something she had to do alone. Taking several unsteady steps, she continued forward, propelled by the need to feel him closer. To know he was truly real and not some sort of vision that came into her life and left.

Caelan had given her back her sense of self. Had made her feel fully like a woman and desirable, not someone to be attacked and used like some sort of expendable item.

When he returned, she vowed to make every single moment between them special.

The door opened to a spacious bedchamber. Straight ahead were double doors with glass windows that opened to a wide balcony. To the right a large four-poster bed flanked by a pair of dark rich wooden tables.

To the left of the doors were an oversized wardrobe and a pair of chairs. The customary screen was set in the far left corner to be used for privacy.

The bedchamber was connected to a smaller room that was currently furnished as a sort of sitting room. She sighed and wondered if Caelan had ever planned for it to be a nursery.

It was the perfect place for her to await his return. He'd mentioned wishing for them to live at the house, once married.

While looking at a beautiful oil painting of a floral vase,

Glynis remembered how she'd argued against living together. Now she could think of nothing else than the good fortune of spending every day with him.

She walked into the adjoining room and sat in one of the chairs. The entire space was him, every piece had obviously been carefully chosen. Like the study, the wood was dark and polished. On the wall was a tapestry depicting a scene with woods and foxes. She wondered if her aunt or his mother had embroidered it.

Her eyes stung with restrained tears and Glynis got to her feet and hurried from the room. Down the corridor, Orla stood with an older woman, who Glynis guessed to be Beatrice's mother.

Indeed, when she neared, she recognized the woman from years earlier when the woman had traveled to Barra to visit family.

"Lady Macdonald, it is good to see ye," Glynis told the woman, who waved away her attempt to curtsy and hugged her.

"Dear girl, I am so very sorry for what is occurring." The woman released her but held her hands. "Like I just told Beatrice and Duncan, Ross men are hardy. Caelan has always been wily as a fox. He will find his way home."

"I pray it is so," Glynis replied her spirits lightened by the woman's words.

"It will be so," Lady Macdonald emphasized. "It is only a matter of when."

Glynis threw herself against the woman and wrapped her arms tightly around her. "Thank ye for helping me feel more assured of his return."

Lady Macdonald's embrace was warm, and the woman smiled widely at her. "I must go see about something for Beatrice to eat." The woman swept around and down the stairs with the grace of a queen.

At the door, Glynis peered in to see her aunt holding a tiny bundle, while Beatrice looked on from the bed. Next to her in a chair was Duncan Ross.

The man was huge and extremely handsome. The hazel gaze moved from his wife to her, and he stood. "Sit and keep her company? I need to see about some things."

Just as he walked past her, he gave her a pointed look. "Do not lose hope."

Glynis swallowed past the lump that formed. "I will not." She lowered to the chair and looked at the sleeping child her aunt lowered for her to see. "She is beautiful."

"I think so as well," Beatrice replied, her gaze shiny. "It is such a bittersweet time. I feel guilty for feeling so happy."

"Ye should not. It is a wonderful thing. A new life. A blessing amidst troubles." She could not help but wonder how it would be the day she gave birth.

Beatrice sniffed. "Duncan is heartbroken and anxious. He wishes to be out there searching for Caelan. At the same time, he does not wish to leave me alone."

It was understandable. There were guards patrolling the house just in case Cairn, who they suspected was responsible for Caelan's disappearance, tried anything else.

"What do ye think?" Glynis asked. "Would it be good for him to go?"

Beatrice nodded. "Aye, I have told him to go. I am well protected."

Just then Isobel and Lady Macdonald walked back inside. Isobel went to the window. "Riders approach. I hope they bring news."

Glynis rushed to look out and indeed a group of horsemen galloped toward the house. "I want to go downstairs and hear what news they bring," she exclaimed.

"I do as well," Isobel said. "One of them is Ewan."

Indeed, one of the horsemen was Ewan Ross, the third in line after Darach.

"It is best we obey Duncan and remain here," Aunt Mariel said although she stretched to look when the men disappeared from their view, riding to the front of the house.

Glynis was not going to wait. She rushed from the room and then down the stairs to the front door.

"What happens?" she called out as she went out to where Ewan dismounted.

His hazel gaze met hers. "There is news. Villagers said they saw a man being dragged into a wagon. They say he was beaten badly, but alive."

"I've come to get ye, Duncan. Ye are the best tracker. There may not be much time and although we've scoured the area, there are no signs that we can find."

Without a word, Duncan turned on his heel and raced into the house.

"We will find him," Ewan stated, his eyes boring into Glynis'. "My brother will come home."

Moments later, Duncan rode away with the men. Glynis watched from the window, unable to move even after they disappeared.

Her entire body ached. It was a surreal feeling that was

caused by the distress she felt at the possibility that Caelan was dying as his family searched for him.

"Ye must eat and rest," her aunt stated. "It is not good for the bairn if ye sink into despair."

"Very well." She allowed herself to be guided down to the front room. The others sat around the table, the food on their plates untouched. It felt sinful to eat and enjoy a good meal while Caelan could be somewhere hungry and thirsty.

"Eat ladies. Otherwise, ye will not be strong enough to care for the mother and child upstairs and Mister Caelan when he returns," Gara, the cook said in a no-nonsense tone that they needed to hear.

The firm instructions seemed to snap them out of their worry, and they all began eating and discussing the logistics of what and where they would remain to await news.

"Since this is closer to where he was last seen, I think we should remain here," her aunt stated. "Besides this is his house."

"We will prepare a recovery room for him in the parlor," Lady Macdonald said. "There will be a need for plenty of bandages."

Glynis spoke next. "Where is the Clan Ross healer now?"

"Waiting at the keep," Isobel replied. "I will send a message asking that he and his helper come here."

Guards rode past the window and Glynis followed their progress. "He should recover here. I agree."

"I will send Agnes and Annis to pack our clothing," Isobel told her and grabbed her hands. "He is coming home."

Tears fell freely. Despite the hopeful tone, there was the underlying fear that Caelan would return home, but not alive.

CHAPTER FIFTEEN

"ACROSS YE say." The old man looked him over. "I suppose those breeches were well-made. What's left of 'em." He laughed at his own joke.

The man pushed a bowl of fish stew in front of Caelan. "Eat. The sooner ye are strong enough, the sooner ye can go."

"Can ye send word? Bring someone here and I will send them to my brother with a message that I am alive."

The old man took his time lowering to a chair. He sniffed the stew. When he smiled, it was evident most of his teeth were either rotted or missing. "I am not bringing no one 'ere to my home."

Caelan closed his eyes. He had to be patient with the wary man. Despite the old man's strange ways, he'd saved his life.

"What about the woman who comes here?"

"Hilda is nothing but a nuisance, she'll forget the message before getting to the rode. Besides, she'll demand payment up-front."

He gave up and began eating. "I will reward ye for this. For saving my life."

THE OLD MAN stood and stretched. "I'll go fetch water to wash up."

It was a long while later that he managed to go outside the

front door. The first few steps had landed him on his back, which had been excruciating.

By the lingering fever, he suspected some of the wounds were festering.

The fact he felt warm and unbalanced confirmed that he was not well. If he didn't find a way home and to proper healing, the rotten wounds would kill him.

The cottage was deep in the forest, not even a clear path was in sight. By the fact it took the old man most of the day to come and go, he figured the nearest creek was not close. Caelan sniffed the air and did not smell the salty breeze of the sea.

Instead, the air smelled of moss, a familiar scent of the forest. He needed to get stronger, so Caelan did his best to walk back and forth in front of the cottage. Within minutes, he was winded and weak.

Dejected he lowered to a bench.

There had to be a way of convincing the old man to get help.

"So ye didna die?" The old woman, Hilda, walked from behind a tree. She waddled on bowed legs to where he sat and fell heavily onto the bench.

"I suppose my days 'ere are coming to an end." She gave him a bleary look. "Any food?"

"Fish stew," Caelan replied.

The woman didn't move. "If ye manage to get away from 'ere, live a good life."

"Can ye help me?" Caelan asked. "I can have a nice cottage built for ye and plenty of food. Make yer last years comfortable."

The woman considered it. "What do ye want me to do? I cannot walk very far."

"Is there someone ye can ask to seek out my family? To give them a message."

The woman stood and went into the cottage. Sounds of rummaging and then the smell of smoke followed by the smell of the fish stew meant she cooked.

He wondered what the relationship was between the two older people. They seemed to have known each other for a long time.

By holding to the wall and doorway, he was able to walk back inside. "Who is he? The man who lives here?"

"Wallace." The woman stirred the pot not looking away. "My brother."

"Where do ye live?"

The woman cackled. "I 'ave no home. He kicked me out years ago. I live where I can."

While she ate, the woman refused to speak to him or answer any more of his questions. That the two people who could help him were so odd and uncooperative frustrated him to the point he was near to losing his temper. It would do no good to scream at the woman or the old man. They were forest people and not used to being around others.

As the woman walked out, she seemed slower. At the doorway, she turned to him. "I will try to help ye."

DUNCAN'S WARHORSE LEAPED over a fallen tree with the grace of a deer. The animal enjoyed a good run and seemed to sense the urgency of their search. Already they'd been out two days in the area where Caelan was reportedly seen.

Hundreds of warriors scoured the woods, questioning everyone they happened across and still nothing helpful was found.

"How can someone disappear? The isle is not so huge that someone could hide so well," Gideon, the youngest Ross sibling asked in an angry tone. "We must find him. We must."

"He is not hiding," Duncan said. "I think he is sick or injured, and unable to get to us."

Just then he caught sight of someone hurrying past some trees. Duncan narrowed his eyes and pulled his horse to a stop. "Did ye see that?"

Gideon shook his head, looking in the direction Duncan did. "What was it?"

"I think it is a person." He urged the steed forward at a slow pace. "Ay! Show yerself," he called out. "We mean ye no harm."

He motioned for Gideon to go to the right as he guided the horse to the left of where he'd seen the person go.

Moments later a woman shrieked as they appeared from both sides. The hag hadn't bathed in a very long time. Dirty stringy hair fell over an alarmed wrinkled face. "Leave me be. I am not a bother to no one." She lowered to the ground and scurried into a lopsided shelter.

Gideon started to dismount, but Duncan motioned for him to stay. He dismounted and bent to peer into the dimness.

"Woman, I will speak to ye from out here," he said lowering to sit on the ground outside the flap of her shelter. "I have coins for ye to buy some food."

"There is no village near here to buy anything. I do not want yer coin. Go away," she replied, in a gruff tone.

Duncan could sense her fear. He understood not trusting people, especially after being mistreated for years. He'd had to learn to not show fear.

"Very well, then I will have someone bring ye food and a blanket. I just require one thing. I am searching for my brother. His name is Caelan. He may be injured or dead."

There was a long silence. "The young man. 'E's not dead."

His heart hammered but he managed to keep his voice even as he exchanged looks with a wide-eyed Gideon.

"Where is he? I must take him home."

"At my brother's. But ye cannot take 'im."

"Where can I find yer brother?"

It was an eternity later that the woman finally came out. She was slow getting up, but finally managed to stand. Duncan ensured to keep his distance so not to frighten her.

Giving him a once over, she frowned. "Ye are a big man." She cackled at the statement seeming not at all intimidated by him. "I will take yer coins. Could find a use for 'em."

Despite the fact she could be lying, he placed a stack of coins in the center of her dirt-caked hand.

"The horses cannot get there. We had to drag 'im on a blanket to see after 'im." The woman began walking with surprising speed for her age and lack of coordination.

Gideon whistled, and a pair of guards appeared. They were instructed to remain with the horses as he and Duncan followed the woman.

There was no clear path to wherever the woman led them, making it clear why they'd not been able to find Caelan in weeks. Several times, she lowered to the ground and crawled through a thicket before going forward. The distance was not long, but upon coming to a dilapidated cottage, Duncan's heart sank. It would be difficult to carry Caelan out and back to the path.

The woman didn't enter, but instead stood outside the door and called in. "Young man, yer brothers are here."

Duncan did not care whose home it was, he burst into the space to find Caelan lying on the floor atop a pile of dirty rags.

"Brother," Caelan said attempting to get up. Duncan did not give him a chance to struggle. He pulled him up and held him against his chest. "We have searched everywhere for ye."

"I know," Caelan said looking up at him.

It was heartbreaking to note all the scars on the usually pristine face, dried blood plastered some of his hair down. When he felt wetness, Duncan realized there were wounds on his back, and they seeped pus.

At once Duncan was transported to what he'd been through and he schooled his expression, fighting not to break down and sob.

When Gideon burst through the door behind him, his brother was not successful and immediately his face turned a sickly green.

"Go outside and wait," Duncan told him as he guided Caelan to sit on a chair.

"The horses cannot get through here and ye are too weak to walk. Gideon and I will have to make a litter to carry ye."

His proud brother nodded and reached for him as if needed to be assured he was truly there. Duncan allowed Caelan to hold his hand for as long as he needed to. The entire time, he assured him that he'd be right back.

"Do not go," Caelan said, his voice cracking with emotion. "Do not leave me."

"Gideon!" Duncan called out and their younger brother appeared at the door. "Go back and get the guards to help. Clear as much of a path as ye can so we can carry him out."

Gideon gave Caelan a pointed look. "I will return soon."

They remained in silence for a long time. Caelan sitting and leaning against Duncan, while he kept vigil. Since his brother did not seem inclined to speak, he would not force him by asking questions. Whatever information needed to be said, they would get it once he got Caelan back home and cared for.

"How did ye do it?" Caelan asked much later, while not moving. "So many years."

Duncan knew his brother referred to the years he'd been in captivity. In truth, the current situation did bring back sensations of impotence and hopelessness that he'd lived with while far away from home.

The many days of hunger and mistreatment had affected him, and instinctively he knew it would be a long time before Caelan would be anywhere close to the man he'd been before being capture.

"I am going to kill Cairn," Duncan told Caelan. "I will not stop until he is dead."

"I have not seen him," Caelan replied then seemed to fall asleep. Duncan did not move, allowing his brother to rest. The trip back to their home would not be long once they figured out how to transport Caelan. They could wait for a wagon, but that could be an entire day.

Gideon returned with one guard and the resourceful young man had a solution.

"We'll carry him to where the horses are. We've acquired a wagon."

Although Duncan and Gideon used their tartans as a litter and to cover him, Caelan had to lay on his stomach to keep his wounds from rubbing against the wooden plats. He moaned a few times when they had to drag the litter through bushes, but for the most part, he did well.

Finally, they reached the wagon. The four guards insisted on removing their cloaks as well to form a more comfortable pallet. Once everyone's clothing was placed onto the wagon bed, Caelan was lifted and laid upon it.

It hurt Duncan to move him as he winced and groaned with the pain of his wounds tearing open, but it couldn't be helped. His brother had a lot more pain in store as the wounds would have to be washed out and cleaned thoroughly.

The sun had fallen, but luckily there was a full moon that gave them enough light to travel to the house.

They rode as quickly as they could without jostling Caelan too much.

"How far?" Caelan asked when Duncan slowed his horse to check on him. His face was wet with perspiration telling of how much pain the movement was bringing. He'd turned to his stomach, but Duncan knew it did not ease the pain much.

"Just a couple more hours. Be strong."

BY THE TIME the wagon slowed, and he realized he had reached his home, Caelan could barely stay coherent.

It was as if his skin was on fire. Every inch of him burning. His mouth was dry despite his brothers constantly giving him water. They'd run out a bit ago, and he'd almost begged for them to stop and find some.

"We are here," Duncan said. "I am going to ask that only mother, Gara, and Firtha be present, he said referring to the cook and housekeeper who'd served them for many years."

"Thank ye," Caelan replied groggily. "I do not wish anyone else to see me." When Duncan hesitated, he took his hand. "Promise me not to allow anyone else to see me."

Duncan nodded in agreement, understanding in his gaze. "I promise."

It seemed a lifetime later that someone climbed onto the wagon and he recognized Creagh, the stableman. Creagh lifted his head and gave him fresh cool water.

"They come now. Yer mother is here as well."

Caelan did his best to prepare for being moved, but he still cried out in pain when it happened.

Moments later he was installed in a bed that had been placed in the downstairs parlor. He heard voices but could not see as he was being carried by his brothers and guards.

"Darling boy," his mother's voice sounded. Her English accented voice strong with pain. "Put him here, we must clean him immediately."

His stepmother's tear-streaked face appeared next. She rubbed his arm. "We are so glad ye are back."

"Everyone must leave the room," the healer ordered. "Duncan, ye and another man may remain."

Duncan and Creagh remained in the room to await instructions from the healer. Gara and Firtha hurried in with pots of boiling water.

The tartan and cloaks that covered him were removed and his breeches cut away. The healer ordered his assistant and the kitchen maids to wash him.

The water was warm and soothing. There were cuts and abrasions on his hands and face that stung when washed, but for the most part it was comfortable. When they turned him to his stomach, the healer placed a strap of leather between Caelan's teeth.

"Bring the bucket of cold water closer, lay the oilcloths upon the floor under here." Caelan shook with a mixture of fear and pain, unable to make out things as everything began to fade.

However, when the first splashes of water, followed by cloths hit his tender skin, he screamed in pain. The leather falling from his mouth.

"What is happening?" Darach arrived and there was a reprieve to the pain. "Stop at once!" he yelled at the healer.

Obviously, his mother and stepmother entered because they began speaking in soothing voices. One stroking his face.

"I will clean his wounds," his stepmother said in a strong voice. "His mother will help him."

Instead of rubbing, his stepmother blotted at his back. It was painful, but not as horrible as the scrubbing.

Little by little they continued, giving him pauses to regain his ability to breathe.

"Caelan," Darach's voice was at his ear. "Be strong. Ye are safe now."

He tried his best but was unable to keep the tears from flowing. Thankfully moments later, the soothing call of unconsciousness claimed him once again.

CHAPTER SIXTEEN

"I MUST SEE him," Glynis stared up at the guards who blocked her way into the parlor where Caelan had been brought several hours earlier.

At first, she'd listened to his mother and aunt, who asked that she remain away until they could see what state he was in. However, upon hearing the screams, she'd hurried to the room.

Unfortunately, the older women had been hurried inside and the guards were given strict orders to keep everyone else out.

She'd caught a glimpse of his foot, but nothing more. The stench of infection and blood had turned her stomach and Glynis had been forced to walk outside until the fresh air settled her.

Now fortified with a cloth that she'd soaked in lavender oil, she was prepared to go in and help. He was her child's father after all.

"Ye cannot pass until we are given orders from the laird." The guard looked past her, his relief evident in his expression.

"Any news?" Isobel asked him.

The man shook his head. "No, my lady. Nothing."

Isobel nodded. "Will ye please knock and tell them we would like to know what happens?"

The guard knocked and moments later the door cracked open and Darach looked out. He walked out carefully closing the door behind him.

"Ye should have sent someone to speak to Glynis and tell her what happens," Isobel scolded. "She is fraught with worry."

When Darach looked to her, he saw that she had indeed been crying. Her nose was red, and her face flushed.

"I was waiting for the healer to explain. Caelan is feverish. He was whipped and the injuries on his back… some of them… have festered. Mother and his mother are cleaning the wounds right now. They are almost finished. Once that is completed, the healer plans to apply an herbal poultice."

"Has he spoken?" Glynis asked, needing to know he was at least coherent.

"Aye, he asked that no one see him until he was cleaned. He's been unable to do much for himself these past days and was filthy."

"What of his injuries?" Glynis asked unable to keep her patience controlled. "What did they do to him?"

Darach shrugged. "I do not know more than what I see. His face is bruised and scarred, there are marks as if he was stabbed on his upper body and his back has been cut by a whip. I do not know more."

They helped her to sit when her knees gave out. She could not imagine what he'd gone through. "When can I see him?" she asked barely able to keep from sobbing.

"It will be best if ye wait until morning. The healer and his helpers will be with him all night. He's already expecting us all to leave the room so he can rest." The laird's tone left no room for argument.

Glynis met his gaze. "Can I just see him? Please. If only for a moment. I need to see him."

The laird seemed to waiver and Isobel stepped in. "She should be allowed to see him."

Finally, the laird nodded. "Let me walk in first."

They followed him to the doorway and Darach walked inside. It was a short while later that the door opened, and her aunt emerged. "Come in. Ye must do yer best to keep from crying or doing anything that will distress him."

Looking around her aunt, she could see that Caelan had been covered with a thin blanket. He lay on his stomach with his head turned to the side and placed on a folded cloth. His hair was wet.

"We washed him, and next the healer will be treating his wounds." Her aunt took her hand and guided her to the bed.

Caelan looked to be asleep. She leaned closer and pressed a kiss to the corner of his mouth. His skin was warm. "Caelan."

When he didn't stir her eyes widened, and she looked to her aunt. "Is he asleep?"

"He was given a tonic to rest. It will help with the treatment of his wounds."

Seeming to understand she needed time, the women and the maids moved away from the bed to stand across the room.

The window was open, probably to allow fresh air to do away with the stench that lingered, and it was making the room quite cold.

Although he looked to be asleep, Caelan was very pale so Glynis touched his face and waited to see if he breathed. He did.

There was a cut just above his right eyebrow and another scar that looked to be healing across his jawline. She wondered how many were on the other side of his face.

"Get better. We have much to speak about," she whispered into his ear and ran her fingers lightly down the side of his face and through his hair. He was alive and it was all that mattered. Glynis blinked away tears when he took a deep breath.

"Get well, my love."

"Miss, I must start the treatment." The healer gave her a pointed look. "Ye must go."

Together with her aunt and his mother, they walked out to the dining room where hot cider was served along with fresh bread, butter, and fruit pudding.

"We have not had the opportunity to be introduced," the older woman with bright blue eyes looked to her. "I am Alberta Roberts, Calean's mother." She had the same English accent as Caelan.

The woman had arrived just moments before the men who brought Calean were sighted, leaving no time for niceties.

"Lady Roberts, I am pleased to make yer acquaintance," Glynis replied feeling very inadequate in that moment. The woman sat ramrod straight, her face impassive and hands folded on her lap.

When she reached for the cup, she lifted it gracefully from the table and took short sips. Glynis couldn't help but watch as she daintily tore a piece of bread and slathered it with just enough butter before nibbling with care.

Her aunt Mariel caught her looking and smiled warmly. "When I first met Alberta, I felt lacking. I had never known anyone so perfect."

Caelan's mother shook her head. "Not so perfect. I carried yer husband's child."

It was interesting that there wasn't any awkwardness between them. The woman had been the late laird's lover and yet her aunt seemed to like her.

Of course, Glynis was aware her aunt never cared for her husband and was probably grateful that the other woman kept him away.

Caelan's mother continued, "And I was in awe of Mariel. How she could run as fast as the wind, and mount and ride a horse without hesitation. While I measured each word and act."

The woman studied Glynis. "Ye are astonishing. A beauty. I can see why my son could not resist ye."

She fought crying with relief that the woman seemed to find her suitable—though Glynis found it hard to believe herself. She sniffed loudly then simply said, "Thank ye."

Alberta smiled. "No need to thank me. I wish we would have met under better circumstances. I have been traveling. My husband and I are going to live in Glasgow."

"I was not aware," Lady Mariel said. "Why?"

The woman's shoulders lifted and lowered. "I have never stopped wishing to return. To be closer to my homeland. Glasgow is a good compromise."

They continued sipping the cider, while Glynis kept watch of the door. "I do not think I can sleep away from here."

Lady Mariel nodded. "We thought ye would feel that way. There are two small bedchambers down the hall from the parlor. Alberta is in one, I will ask the other be prepared for ye."

"Sleep well, morning will come soon enough. We should have a better idea of how Caelan fares." His mother stood and went into the parlor.

Glynis followed her progress. "Will the healer allow her to remain?"

"He wouldn't dare contradict her," her aunt replied. "Ye look dead on yer feet." She stood and went to find someone to set up the small bedroom.

A SOUND WOKE Glynis and she sat up disoriented, unsure of where she was. It was a few moments before she recalled that she was at Caelan's house.

Moans sounded and she slipped from the bed. Once she donned a robe, she walked out of the room, and opening the door slowly, she tiptoed into the parlor.

Lady Roberts stood next to the bed where a disheveled Caelan sat. His hands rested on the mattress as he slid to the side of the bed until his legs hung over the side. With each movement, he moaned in pain.

"Mother, ye should leave. I do not want anyone seeing me like this."

"I will not leave until I am assured ye are recovered," she replied calmly. "I should seek the healer to come."

"No," he said looking up at her. "Do not."

For a long moment, he sat without moving, his chest heaving with each breath. "I hurt all over," he murmured. "What did he do?"

"The wounds were festering, we had to scrub them raw to ensure they were thoroughly cleaned. Do ye not remember?" his mother asked.

"I remember feeling as if being torn apart. Aye."

"Caelan," Glynis took a step forward. "Ye are awake."

His gaze traveled over her hesitating on her stomach. His expression turned hard, and he looked to his mother. "Send her away."

"Caelan," Glynis repeated. "I wish to allow yer mother to rest for a bit. I can sit with ye."

"I prefer to be alone." He did not look at her, but once again spoke to his mother. "Please take her away from me."

What he said did not make sense to her and Glynis took another step closer. Was he hallucinating? Perhaps still feverish?

"Please go," Alberta blocked her son from view. "I am sorry. But it is best not to upset him."

Not waiting to hear more, she whirled and hurried back out into the corridor. Why did he not want to see her?

Mind awhirl, she returned to her small chamber and lit a lantern. Then she paced. After a long while, she climbed into bed to attempt to get sleep. Surely the next morning, after the sun rose, Caelan's mind would clear and he'd call for her.

Unfortunately, she could not close her eyes without picturing how he'd kept his gaze from her. The words he'd uttered to his mother repeating in her head over and over.

By the time morning came, she could not wait to speak to her aunt about what had occurred. Surely, together they would come up with a solution. Speak to Caelan and find out why he was upset.

Did he blame her for what happened to him? It had nothing to do with her, so it was not possible. Unless of course, his mind was not well. It could be the fever had affected him.

It seemed a lifetime before she heard voices in the dining room. Praying Caelan's mother was not at first meal, she left the bedchamber. Sitting at the table were Isobel, Lady Macdonald, Darach, and her aunt.

Glynis lowered to the empty chair, which was next to her aunt.

"Should we send for Alberta?" her aunt asked the room in general.

Isobel shook her head. "I sent Annis to check on her just a bit ago and she is fast asleep in her bedchamber. So let her rest."

"Who is with Caelan?" Glynis blurted out the question.

"Gara is," her aunt replied. "She is feeding him. Duncan is also there."

Glynis turned to look at the door.

"Have ye been to see him?" It was Darach who asked, which made her uncomfortable. She'd not planned to tell anyone other than her aunt about Caelan's reaction to her.

"Yes. I did last night." Glynis looked at her aunt. "He asked me to leave." Her voice caught on the last word.

Everyone was silent for a beat. Since she was looking down at the table, it was possible they were exchanging looks to see who would say something.

"I will go see him and find out what happens. It could be he is embarrassed. Caelan has always been proud of his appearance," Darach said.

"This is not a time to be proud," Isobel said, pinning her husband. "We should ensure he is not being coerced."

When Glynis gave her aunt a questioning look, her aunt lowered her tone to a soft whisper. "Alberta can be a bit… em, selective about who her sons marry. She is not aware of the fact ye are with child. So perhaps, she is attempting to convince Caelan to find another wife. However, I sincerely doubt it."

"I will speak to him. I am the mother of his child and do not need others to intercede for me. If it does not go well, then I will ask for yer help."

She pushed from the table and stood straight, hoping to convey assurance while her stomach clenched. The closer Glynis got to the door, the harder her heart thudded. What if he had indeed changed his mind about marrying her?

"I will return with Creagh in a short while to help ye. Ye should not stay seated too long. The healer expects for ye to remain abed." Gara walked out.

The woman saw Glynis and walked to the door with a tray. "Be strong," she whispered on her way past.

Upon seeing her, Duncan glanced at his brother and then to her. There was a blank expression on his face as he walked out past her.

Caelan did not notice her at first. He was laying on his side, staring out the window. When she neared, his eye barely shifted to her. "Please leave."

"I will not. I wish to help. We should talk."

He closed his eyes and let out a long breath as if steeling himself. "There is nothing that needs to be said. I wish ye to leave."

Her heart shattered at seeing him so broken. It was obvious he tried to keep from her how much he suffered.

"Caelan, I've been attacked, I understand. My injuries were not as...," she could not put a word to the horrible things that he'd gone through. "I was not as badly injured. I cannot imagine…"

When he looked to her, there was something in his eyes, as if pleading. "I need ye to walk out and not say another word."

Jaw tight, he swallowed visibly. "Perhaps another day we can speak. Right now, I cannot be in the same room with ye."

Glynis' sharp intake of breath was the only sound in the room as the words cut through her, like daggers. As much as she tried to understand that he was reacting out of pain, a part of her could not help but be upset that he did not wish her near.

"Why?"

He didn't reply but instead kept his gaze straight out the window.

"I was sick with worry and praying for yer return. Allow me to help, please. I wish to be here, with ye. Do not push me away."

"Guard!" he called out.

The door opened and Darach walked in. "What happens?"

"Take her out of here," Caelan said in a voice that sounded fierce and hollow at the same time.

Darach looked to his brother and seemed to see something she did not. He hurried to her. "Come." He took her by the shoulders and not giving her a choice, guided her out the door and then slammed it behind her.

Before she could turn, the lock sounded.

One shaky step in front of the other, she walked back to the bedchamber. This had to be temporary. He did not wish for her to see him suffering. It could be more than that, she understood as at times, the attack she'd been through seemed to have just happened.

For Caelan everything was raw. It would be a long time before he would be himself again.

If ever.

CHAPTER SEVENTEEN

As soon as the lock on the door engaged, Caelan let out a shaky breath and panted as he fought against the intense spasms that tightened across his back.

Darach came to the bed and lifted him to sit. He let out a loud moan at the pain the movement caused. Then sitting on the bed, he clung to his older brother and sobbed.

"I . . . cannot . . . withstand . . . it," he said, barely able to pronounce each word. "I would almost prefer death to this. Please keep them all out."

Darach was silent, allowing him to cry as his back continued the horrible assault. Suddenly the spasms stopped, a short-lived reprieve based on how they'd come and gone since before daybreak.

Breathing heavily, he took the wet cloth Darach gave him and mopped his face. Too exhausted to do more than remain hunched over, he allowed new tears to stream down his face.

Never in his life had he ever suffered so. And with each pain, his heart broke more and more for Duncan, who'd been whipped repeatedly while being held captive for years.

"How did he do it?" he asked Darach, who stood at the window arms crossed. His face was etched with worry as he looked to him.

"After a while, ye learn to distance yerself from pain. He

told me once that for days he'd be in an imaginary place and that gave him solace."

Caelan grimaced and stood, needing to be out of the bed. He wore only a pair of loose-fitting braies that fell past his knees. The healer had to pull them down when cleaning his wounds since some of the whippings had gone as low as the top of his buttocks.

"Our mothers will want to be here to see about ye."

"I cannot allow it," Caelan said. "Gara, the healer, and my brothers only."

There was understanding in his brother's expression. "I will explain it to them."

"I prefer ye do not disclose the reason to Glynis."

"She should know…"

"No. I will not appear weak before her."

"Ye are a Ross through and through, ye are not weak. A lot has happened. Give yerself time brother."

"I am asking ye as my brother to not betray my trust." Caelan felt the first twinge and his breath caught. "Promise me."

As he expected, there was no hesitation. Since young, he and his brothers had always quickly made promises. It was the one thing they'd kept through the years.

"I promise."

When the next set of spasms hit, once again he clung to his brother and moaned.

"Ye can cry or scream," Darach said. "There is nothing worse than attempting to be strong when there is no strength left."

His moans were loud and soon there was pounding on the

door. "Darach, let me in." It was his stepmother. "I will see to him."

It was a while longer until the spasms stopped, and he could catch his breath. "Tell her to please go."

"Ye should have someone in here with ye. Not be alone until the healer returns."

Caelan could barely keep his eyes open. "Very well. Stepmother."

Once Darach helped him to lay on his side, he let out short breaths as the pain subsided. "I will stay here for a bit longer. I will send for Ewan and Stuart to come. We will take turns staying in here with ye."

Moments later, he heard whispering and when he opened his eyes, his stepmother sat next to the bed. "Darach went to send for yer brothers. Other than Duncan and Ewan, who are hunting that horrible person down, the others will be staying here."

Just as he was about to talk the spasms came over him. "The…door."

"It is locked," his stepmother assured him as sobs and pain rocked through him.

IT WAS LATE one day and Caelan was barely coherent. Between the spasms, the pain of his wounds being cleaned, and the throbbing headache, he couldn't think clearly. His throat was sore from crying out and his entire body shook.

"There has to be something we can do to ease the spasms," one of his brothers demanded. Caelan wasn't sure who. Earlier that day, Stuart had spent most of the afternoon with him, but he'd lost track of time.

"I have tried everything. Whoever whipped him cut deep and that is causing it. When the injury heals the spasms should stop."

"He cannot withstand much more!" Caelan realized it was Gideon, the youngest who was making the loud demands. "He is out of his mind."

After a moment, a wet cloth was placed over his back. The cold seeped into his body and it felt oddly calming. "Hopefully this will help." The healer sounded calm despite Gideon yelling at him.

"Gideon," Caelan said, and his brother's angelic face appeared before him.

"Is it helping?" Gideon asked.

"A bit," he replied praying it helped stop the spasms.

They waited a while and just as the cloth warmed, once again his back began to tighten.

"We must change the cloth at once," the healer said to someone.

When a cold cloth was placed on his back, Caelan inhaled sharply at the cold. But he would rather that, a hundred times more, than the pain of the spasms.

After a while, they found a rhythm that worked. Wet cloth, fanning his skin, allowing it to warm just enough, and replacing the cloths.

He was able to sleep, waking only occasionally when a cold cloth was placed on his back.

WHILE CAELAN ATE, his mother sat in a chair watching him. "I am still angry that ye would not allow me in here for days."

"I understand," Caelan replied. He shifted awkwardly since the fabric of the tunic he wore grazed over his back. Despite being bandaged, he felt every single move.

"Ye look better," she admitted. "Yer coloring has returned."

"When do ye leave?" he asked because he needed her to keep to her plans and not stall because of him. "I am healing and promise to come visit soon."

His mother gave him a knowing look. "Have I overstayed my welcome?"

"Of course not, Mother."

"I will prepare to leave on the morrow. I have to finish looking over the packing. Otherwise, my husband will take over and I will be unable to find things for years."

He took her in. Still beautiful despite the graying temples, she was an elegant woman who, to this day, spoke with a flawless English accent. How she'd fallen for a man like his father, Caelan would never understand.

Despite having a child born out of wedlock, she'd managed to marry well to a wealthy man who doted on her. Caelan had two other half brothers—a product of their marriage—who were much younger than him and were now just reaching their twenties.

He'd not spent as much time with them as he'd hoped. Once he returned from boarding schools as a young man of ten and five, his father had demanded Caelan live at Ross Keep. Therefore, he was much closer to his paternal half siblings.

HIS BROTHERS, DARACH, Stuart, and Gideon gathered the next day, in the parlor where he slept. They sat in chairs near the large window past which a gloomy sky and mist appeared. Winter had arrived and with it a bleak scene outside.

Caelan adjusted in the chair, careful not to lean back. A pillow had been placed in the small of his back that helped him sit upright and not hurt his wounds.

"He is close, I can feel it," Stuart insisted. "He could not have gone far. I am hard-pressed to believe he left South Uist."

Darach shrugged. "If he had prepared for someone to wait for him before leaving his village, he could have gone straight there and boarded one of the many bìrlinns for hire."

Anton, Stuart's squire, had seen Cairn in a village near the southern shore. However, when guards had arrived in search, he was gone.

"He is hiding. We will find him. I will kill him," Stuart's statement was flat, without emotion and Caelan believed him.

However, Cairn had better hope any one of his brothers find him besides Duncan. At least he'd have a swift death if another of them found him first.

AS THEY DISCUSSED the logistics and number of guards that had been dispatched to every isle and region, he couldn't help but think of Glynis.

He'd sent her away and she'd not returned. For days he'd thought about how he'd reacted to her presence, but he could not ever face the woman he loved while crying like a babe and clinging to one of his brothers begging they knock him out.

When Duncan had come to spend time with him, he'd not hesitated and punched him so hard, he'd been unconscious for hours. When he'd come to, Darach was chastising Duncan, and he had not been allowed to stand watch over Caelan again.

Caelan had managed to laugh about it.

"I want to ride out to search," Caelan said looking at his brothers. "I want to be there when he dies."

"Ye will be there," Darach affirmed. "We will bring him here."

They were silent for a long moment and then Darach stood and stretched. "We have not heard from Ewan. It has been two days. It could be there is good news."

"Who went with him?" Caelan asked.

Darach gave him a knowing look. Wherever Ewan was if Artair was along, they would track whoever hid until finding them. They were a tenacious pair.

Later as they sat drinking ale and keeping him company, there was a knock and Gideon opened it to Artair. Their cousin was caked in mud from his head to his boots. He sported a wide grin.

"We got him."

Caelan got to his feet ignoring the pain that although lesser than days before, still hurt. "Where is he?"

"Here, of course," Artair said strolling in and waiting for Gideon to lock the door. "We half dragged him here. He is a sobbing mess. Begging for mercy."

TOGETHER THEY WALKED out, past the women who tried to follow them, but were held back by guards who were instructed to block them from the doors.

Knowing his stepmother and the others, they would be watching from the windows. Caelan had no idea what they'd see. Would his stepmother wish for him to spare Cairn's life and instead have him locked in the dungeon for the rest of his life? That would be a horrible fate.

But the last time he'd been imprisoned, he had bribed his way out. Cairn was too wily to keep imprisoned for long.

The fact his mind was racing in so many directions worried him. Why was he considering being merciful?

Stuart stood next to Cairn who was on his knees gasping for breath. His clothes were torn, and he bled from his nose and arms. Artair had not been lying about half-dragging him by the look of it.

When seeing him, Cairn cried out. "Ye live. I am glad for it."

Fury raced through his veins as he stared at the man who struggled to stand but was pushed back down by Stuart.

"I did not wish ye to be killed," Cairn said then looked to Darach. "I specifically told the guards not to kill any of ye. I have known ye since ye were wee lads." The man crawled to Darach's feet. "Do ye not see?"

Darach took a step back. "What I see is a man who despite being like a second father to us, betrayed our trust. Not once, but over and over again. I needed ye Cairn. Ye were to be my advisor."

The man howled as if beaten. "I am sorry. Anything ye wish. Just say it."

Darach's nostrils flared, and he looked to Caelan. "What say ye brother? What is this traitor's fate?"

Indeed, the man had seen them grow up and had interceded often on their behalf with their abusive father.

"Why do ye hate us so?"

Cairn looked to him. There was a flicker of what seemed to be dislike, but he quickly masked it. "I wished for more than just to be a dog that was ordered about. I wanted the seat of laird. I deserved it. I…"

There was a look of shock as the end of a blade pierced through his right side.

"Ye do not deserve to live," Duncan said.

Their large brother had somehow materialized without any of them hearing or seeing him. Obviously, they'd been too focused on Cairn and not paying attention.

Cairn gasped and placed his hands over the wound. "Please. I will do anything."

When his brothers looked to Caelan, he walked closer to the man. "I believe ye."

The injured man sagged with relief. "Thank ye."

"I believe ye will do anything to destroy us," Caelan said and held out his hand to Duncan, who gave him the broad sword. "Ye are a poison."

Caelan swung the sharp blade with all the strength he could muster and cut across the man's throat who'd caused his family so much pain and suffering.

Hands around his throat, the man looked at him with disbelief and then fell forward.

From the second story window, the women looked down as he swayed on his feet. When he met his stepmother's gaze, there was pride in her expression.

He then searched for another face, but there was only Isobel and Lady Macdonald at the window.

"Let us go inside and celebrate," Artair said holding up his sword. "Perhaps we can have peace for a long time now."

"Just in time for the Hogmanay celebrations," Gideon said giving Caelan an approving nod.

As if conjured by the God to show their approval. Snow began falling. Flakes fluttered down over them and would soon cover the ground, hiding the red puddle of Cairn's blood.

His brothers helped him inside, while guards dragged the corpse away.

"Bury him at Keep Ross," Darach called out. "In the family cemetery."

No one protested. After all, their father who'd betrayed them all was also buried there. Cairn was family. He'd lived with them all his life and would remain there now.

"What are ye thinking?" Duncan walked beside him and stopped when Caelan hesitated.

Caelan looked up at the sky and then to the house. "Will I ever be the same again?"

His brother studied him for a long moment. "No. Ye will not. But ye will heal and over time will become who ye are meant to be."

"I feel worse now about what ye went through Duncan. I cannot imagine it. How horrible yer life was."

"There were many times I tried to kill myself. To jump overboard and drown. Every time something or someone impeded it. One time I managed to jump, but I was tied to a post by my ankle. They left me hanging there an entire day until I passed out." Duncan had the audacity to chuckle. "I thought I'd died. When I came to, I was very disappointed."

Caelan shook his head. "What about now? How do ye feel?"

"The darkness follows, but over time it has lessened. With

my beautiful wife, this home, my family, and now the wee lass, I am happy."

Caelan smiled. "Aye, ye are."

CHAPTER EIGHTEEN

"CAIRN IS DEAD," her aunt announced to the room where she and the other woman gathered.

"What will ye do now?" Isobel asked her. It seemed to be the daily question that someone asked her. "Ye could speak to Caelan…"

"No," Glynis replied adamantly. "I will not speak to him." She looked to her aunt. "I wish to return with Cait and Stuart when they leave and take their offer of living there."

Her aunt nodded. "I agree that ye can live there, it is a good place. However, ye more than anyone understands what Caelan is going through. Be patient. He will come for ye."

Isobel looked between them. "Do ye plan to marry Caelan?"

"I do not," Glynis said. "If it were meant to be, it would be. I will not spend my days in wait."

In truth, any affection she'd felt for him remained strong, while at the same time, she'd managed to secure it away. A hollow sensation took over whenever she thought of him. She'd refused to look out the window preferring not to see him.

"I believe once the Hogmanay celebration ends, everyone will head to their prospective homes," Isobel said. "Darach and I will return to Keep Ross today. I am sure Beatrice is ready to have her home back."

Glynis was relieved. "May I return with ye?"

"I will go as well," her aunt said. "Annis, find Agnes and pack up our things. We will leave within the hour."

The young woman got up and stretched. "I look forward to sleeping in my own bed."

Moments later, Orla, Beatrice's handmaid appeared. "Mister Caelan wishes to speak to ye." She looked from Glynis to her aunt. "Both of ye."

"Tell him I will be there shortly, and that Glynis is asleep."

Her aunt gave her a knowing look.

"Perhaps they should speak," Isobel said looking worried.

Before Glynis could say anything her aunt cut in. "Not once has Caelan asked to see Glynis, nor inquired about her well-being. She is expecting his child and understandably he wishes to know how she fares. However, she is not prepared for it."

"Thank ye," Glynis said and took a deep breath. It felt good to be understood and supported. As much as she wanted to speak to Caelan, she was truly not ready. Perhaps it was selfish of her, then again, both of them had so much healing ahead.

It was a whirlwind and soon everything was ready. The carriage was loaded and prepared for Glynis and her aunt to return to the keep.

"Let us go see Beatrice," her aunt said.

"Aunt Mariel and I are returning to the keep with Isobel and Darach," Glynis said to Beatrice who met her gaze with understanding. "I wished to thank ye for the hospitality and to see the beautiful lassie one more time."

Beatrice smiled. "I will be coming to the keep for Hogmanay. So ye will see more of her." The pretty woman let out a sigh. "I am so sorry that ye are hurt by Caelan's actions. I would be furious as well. However, understand that he's been through so much."

"I am no longer angry and have accepted things. Caelan is not ready for many things, not after what happened to him and I understand. In all honesty, I look forward to raising this wee one along with Cait and Stuart's."

For a long moment, Beatrice studied her. "I can see that ye are fully at peace and I am glad for it."

Once in the corridor, Glynis looked from one side to the other. She'd become adept at moving around the house and avoiding the Ross men. It wasn't that she was angry with them, more that she did not want them to try to defend their brother's actions. Partly she understood that she should be patient with Caelan, while at the same time, her feelings were deeply hurt that he refused to see her.

She let out a breath when Duncan came around the corner from downstairs. He hesitated and met her gaze. "How fare ye?"

"Well," she replied. "Aunt Mariel and I return to the keep."

"I understand." His reply was surprising.

Skirting around him, she hurried the way he'd come and down the stairs. She hesitated and looked down the corridor to where Caelan slept. He'd yet to be moved upstairs, but it was only a matter of days. He was better able to walk from what her aunt had told her and gaining strength daily.

"Glynis."

The sound of his voice seemed to cut through her, and she shivered from the assault of emotions that struck at once.

He was in the great room. She'd not expected it since he usually kept to the parlor.

Her pulse racing, Glynis hesitated, not turning to face him. She'd done well in pushing away how he looked, and how his presence made her feel. It would not do to see him again.

"Just one moment is all I ask."

Taking a full breath, she whirled to face him.

He was leaner, his face unshaven and hair longer. And yet, he remained the same aristocratic man she remembered.

"I understand. I needed time to…"

"Ye do not need to make any excuses. I understand. Ye have been through a horrible ordeal." She walked closer to him. "Ye need time alone to heal fully and I need to be away so that I do not take it personally. The bairn and I will be well. It is better this way."

An expression of disbelief transformed his face. His gaze bore into her. "Ye do not mean it."

"I do. Once the bairn is born, ye can visit him or her. I will ensure the child knows his father. It is best that we accept that fate does not wish for us to be together. I wish ye well Caelan and pray for your complete healing."

Remaining silent, after a moment, his gaze fell.

As she walked out of the house, she changed her mind about not seeing him. She was glad they'd spoken, and she could face him and confirm that indeed she still loved him, but the ability to keep her heart protected was firmly in place.

"I HAVE THE perfect bedchamber for ye," her aunt said as they rode back. "It overlooks the garden and has a small balcony where ye can get fresh air."

"It is only for a few weeks," Glynis said. "I will be leaving with Cait and Stuart just after the Hogmanay celebration."

Her aunt gave her a sad look. "I agree that ye should go, but I will miss ye."

"Ye will be coming to visit often. I see how ye are with all the bairns. How ye divide yer time to ensure to see them all often."

They were silent as her aunt seemed to be considering how she would accomplish it all. "My goodness when Gideon has children and Ella… I am not sure I will be in one place for long."

CHAPTER NINETEEN

THE CRACK OF the whip echoed in his ears, the horrific feeling of his skin splitting open followed by the sharp sting made Caelan arch his back, attempting in vain to distance himself from the next assault. But it was of no avail and the second crack brought an involuntary scream that filled the room waking him up.

His breathing was more like wheezing as he tried to inhale deeply. Praying no one had heard him. He sat with his legs over the side of the bed doing his best to push away the nightmare.

It had been several days since the last one. Each time it was different, but just as real. Caelan stood and walked to the window, pushing the curtains aside to look out to the darkness.

The sky was alight with stars and automatically he began searching for constellations he'd learned about from the scholars at the school he'd attended in Glasgow.

Was Glynis awake? He searched the ground below and wondered if she would have liked the garden there. It was probable she'd prefer to live closer to the sea. He'd learned from his stepmother that Glynis had grown up by the sea in Barra.

Perhaps she had been right in that they needed to be apart?

In truth, between the horrible dreams and healing, he was of no use to anyone at the moment. At the same time, he thought of her constantly and fought not to seek her out.

Once Hogmanay was over, she planned to return with Stuart and Cait and live there. Interesting that she'd spoken about it and was what she'd planned since they'd been there.

His lips curved at recalling how she'd informed him of her plans, her green gaze bright and expression sincere.

Glynis was the woman for him, they were meant to be together, but the rift between them seemed insurmountable at the moment. She'd made peace with living separate lives, and had no qualms about raising their bairn alone.

Over and over, he'd questioned if he should have allowed her to be in the room while he recovered. But he could not even consider her witnessing the way he'd suffered and cried like a babe at the pain assaulting him. No man wanted the woman they loved to witness them at their weakest, at their worst.

Caelan closed his eyes and pictured Glynis' face. The woman was beautiful, perfect even. She was with child. His child.

Straightening he let out a long breath. No matter what, he could not allow it, for his son or daughter to be born and raised fatherless. He would fight for his family.

DUNCAN WAS NEVER a talkative person. And like most mornings, they broke their fast with little to say. They sat on one end of the long wooden table, across from each other. As was their custom, they sat in the chairs closest to the kitchens.

"It is like old times," Gara said entering with a tray of food. "Just the two of ye."

"Beatrice prefers to remain upstairs for now, and her mother joins her for first meal," Duncan replied.

When Gara walked out Caelan met Duncan's gaze. "I am going to Keep Ross. I will stay there for a while."

"I am surprised it took ye this long," Duncan replied.

His brother gave him a pointed look. "I understand why ye kept away from her. We can run away, but we will never outrun the nightmares brother. Ye will have to learn to live with them and hopefully over time, they will become further apart."

Caelan nodded. "I am not sure there is a way to repair the rift between Glynis and I."

"Possibly not, but ye will not know for sure unless ye try to win her back." With an uncharacteristic grin, Duncan leaned forward. "Ye are a charmer, put it to good use."

"Never thought to get romantic advice from ye," Caelan replied getting up from the table.

Duncan frowned. "Strange what love does to a man."

After wrapping himself in a thick tartan, he walked outside and waited for Creagh, who brought his horse. The man gave him a once over. "It is good to see ye out."

"It is good to be able to walk without swaying," Caelan said. "See that my trunk is taken to Keep Ross. I hope to see ye at Hogmanay."

Mounting felt strange, but Caelan was determined to get stronger. It was strange how spending weeks recovering made it so hard to feel normal again.

His wounds had healed, although from what he could see in the looking glass, they'd left angry raised scars that time would soothe, but not completely erase.

In a way the scarring did not bother him, it was the reminder he'd have of fighting to live, for the rest of his life of the ordeal.

The sky was clear for it being winter. After raining for several days, it was a welcome reprieve. Longing for salty air, he planned to ride along the shore and take the long way to the keep. The preparations were beginning for the Hogmanay celebration and he looked forward to aggravating Greer, the cook, by visiting the kitchens often.

The ride was good. However, by the time the keep came into view, he was tiring. Both his back and legs ached, but he welcomed it. He planned to ride daily to get his body accustomed to the activity once again.

The salty air filled his lungs, the call of seabirds above soothing to his mind. Caelan pulled his horse to a stop and allowed his gaze to travel across the view before him. To the right the waves crashed against the shore, as if daring anyone to come near. To the left was a long inlet with softer waves that curved delicately just below the hills where Keep Ross stood.

The cool breeze blew across the inlet bending tall reeds sideways as if bringing messages from the sea.

His horse pawed the ground and lowered its head to graze as Caelan gathered his thoughts. All his life he'd lived there, in the eastern shore of the isle. Except for the four years he'd gone away to study in Glasgow.

Now he wondered what the future held. As bookkeeper for the laird, how would Darach react to him wishing to move closer to Stuart and Cait? Because wherever Glynis and his child went, so would he.

Just then his brother exited the keep gates and walked across the hilly ground with his dog. The animal raced in front and circled back, its excited barks carrying to where Caelan was.

He urged the horse closer until the dog saw him and began barking in warning. The hair on its back raised as he stood in front of Darach, protecting his master.

"It's me Albie," Caelan called out and dismounted.

Upon recognizing his voice, the animal raced to greet him, tail wagging and tongue lolling from the side of its mouth.

Caelan scratched the animal behind the ears until it deemed it enough and raced to find a branch to bring back to play fetch.

"Brother." Darach smiled in a way that Caelan recognized as the laird being in a good mood.

He released the horse to graze. "I needed to come. I plan to remain here for the Hogmanay celebration and perhaps longer."

"This is yer home, there is no need to inform me of yer plans." Darach laughed when the dog dragged a huge branch toward them. "He never gives up. No matter the challenge," his brother said giving Caelan a pointed look.

"I have waited too long, haven't I?" Caelan let out a long breath. How he loved the smell of the sea. It was only because he didn't want to continue living with their father and witness the cruelty that he'd left the keep. Later he remained away because of Duncan. His brother needed someone there with him.

Darach placed a hand on his shoulder. "Ye have been through an ordeal I cannot imagine. Everyone understands why ye have kept away. I do not agree that ye remained away from Glynis for so long. But like ye, I made a stupid mistake once, and almost lost Isobel because of it. If ye love her, then ye will have to work hard to gain her love again."

"How is she?"

The laird leaned down broke a smaller branch and tossed it and Albie raced to retrieve it. "She is well. Seems happy and spending a great deal of time in the kitchen. Isobel says Glynis has asked Greer to teach her to cook her favorites."

A strange feeling of nervousness filled him. It was childish to feel that way about entering his childhood home, but he couldn't stop it. "I best go in," he said, the words sounding like a question rather than a statement.

Darach didn't reply, instead he waved him off and ran after the dog. It was the laird's daily routine that he'd done since young. Darach loved dogs and often collected several of them. Currently, he only had one and spent several hours a day out walking with the happy animal.

As Caelan rode through the gates, the guard called out greetings. He couldn't help but grin when one waved with both arms from atop the wall.

"Oy, cousin. 'Tis about time ye come around." It was Artair. With the huge bow and quiver across his back, he walked closer and peered down. "Have ye tried to shoot an arrow yet? Want to try it?"

Caelan chuckled. "Later, aye. Not sure how good I will be."

"Ye never were any good at it. But it will be good to stretch yer back." Artair crouched down and studied him. "Ye look good. Pale, but good."

"If ye are trying to have yer way with me, flowery words will not work. I prefer whiskey," he called back.

At his cousin's barks of laughter, Caelan couldn't help but chuckle.

A pair of lads greeted him, waiting to take his mount. One looked up at him, the freckled face lad looked to be about ten and five. "Yer trunk was delivered a few moments ago, Mister Caelan."

"Thank ye," he replied. "I do not know ye. What is yer name?"

"Bram, sir," the lad replied. "I am son of Athol, the baker at the village."

Caelan met the young man's gaze for a bit. Something about him touched him, the earnest desire to be of help and the bright reaction to Caelan speaking to him. "I am glad to meet ye," he finally said and remained standing for a moment before walking inside.

There had been plenty of time for someone to alert Glynis of his presence. He'd purposely taken his time arriving and entering to keep from surprising her. It was best that she don her armor and be prepared for him to be there.

What she probably wasn't aware of was that he planned to remain this time. The last time he'd given up too easily. Tried to speak to her and then returned to his house. Not this time.

The great room was busy. Ewan sat at the highboard looking on as two men complained, yelling at one another. Caelan almost laughed when Ewan looked over to him and waved.

His brother would wait for the duo to realize he was not going to speak to them while they argued.

Caelan walked to the highboard and sat next to his brother. It seemed the men were arguing over sheep constantly getting into the fields of the other and eating his grain. It was understandable for the farmer to be angry. What didn't make sense is why the sheepherder was.

"He killed two sheep and his family had a grand feast," Ewan explained.

"Ah," Caelan said before nodding at the servant who poured ale and placed a cup in front of him.

While the men argued, he scanned the room. Over by the fireplace away from all the commotion were a trio of women and bairns of several ages. Some toddled attempting to walk, while a younger one crawled. Glynis sat in a chair knitting, while Catriona, Ewan's wife, sat on the floor with the crawler. In another chair was Isobel. His stepmother was not there, and he wondered where she was.

"Where is Stuart?" he asked Ewan, who scanned the room.

"I do not know."

"What about Stepmother?"

"Probably in the kitchen. I believe Uncle Angus and Aunt Iona are arriving soon to spend the Hogmanay here with us."

"Artair must be glad not to have to travel between here and his parent's home to celebrate with both families."

Just then the herder swung and punched the farmer, who toppled backward and fell across a table.

Everyone in the room stopped talking and turned to see what happened. It was then Caelan realized Glynis had not been aware of his presence.

Her eyes widened at seeing him. For a scant moment, their eyes locked before she turned to look over her shoulder.

Probably seeking a way to escape. He would not approach her.

Forcing his attention away from her, he spoke to the herder.

"Why did ye hit him?"

"He roasted two of my sheep and had the gall to invite me to come and eat." The man spat out the words, his face turning an alarming shade of red. "I want him to pay for it and replace my sheep."

When Caelan looked to Ewan, his brother's right eyebrow lifted in challenge.

The farmer regained his stance. "He owes me more than two sheep for all the damage his deranged animals caused."

"Stop speaking," Caelan shouted, his deep voice causing the men to freeze and look between him and Ewan.

"A shepherd's purpose is to look over his flock and keep them safe," Caelan said meeting the herder's gaze. "Ye failed to keep yer sheep from harm. Now ye expect this man to pay for yer lack of responsibility?"

The man glared at the farmer. "He killed them."

The farmer seemed uncertain when he spoke. "It was my right. They were in my fields."

"Ye are right," Caelan said. "But this man is yer neighbor. Yer duty is to keep watch over yer fields, to ensure the plants grow and produce grain for the clan. Ye failed as a farmer and as a neighbor."

The confused men looked to one another and then back to him. "What do ye expect us to do?" the farmer asked. "I cannot stand out in my field all day and night."

"I cannot keep watch all day and night," the shepherd said almost repeating what the other one said.

"In that ye are both right," Caelan said. "That is why as members of this clan, we help one another." He met each man's gaze. "Dogs would keep sheep from harm and will protect land boundaries if trained and treated well."

After a long moment, a man called out from the back of the room. "I have well-trained dogs and pups that will soon be old enough to work for ye."

"Do not return to me with the same complaints," Ewan stated, his gaze going to the back of the room as Darach walked in and gave the two men a scorching look.

The men hurried to find the man who had dogs.

"That was a good idea, what made ye think about it?" Ewan asked watching the trio of men begin to haggle over the price for the dogs.

"Darach and his dog. Just before I came in, he was out there spending time with the dog. The dog protected him until recognizing me."

When noticing that Glynis walked out and went toward the kitchen, he stood and followed. She wasn't in the corridor, or in the kitchens. When he walked out, he saw that she was in the garden standing near the shed with her arms around herself to keep warm.

Thankfully he had his plaid, so he neared and placed it over her shoulders. Glynis bristled, but did not remove it. "I am not prepared to speak to ye." Her voice trembled just enough to let him know she was as nervous as he was.

"Then listen to me," he replied. When she didn't turn, he hated to not look at her face. However, the fact she remained gave him a glimmer of hope.

"I will never be able to convey why I kept away from ye.

Never was it my intent to hurt ye. It was more to protect myself."

"There is no need for explanation," Glynis replied. "I understand yer reasons although I wish ye would have allowed me to be with ye."

"I beg for yer forgiveness."

When she did not reply, he continued. "Glynis, marry me. My intent is to give ye a home, wherever ye wish to live and for us to raise our child together. That he or she grow up with two parents who love him dearly."

"I cannot," Glynis dropped the tartan and rushed from the garden.

Caelan bent to pick up the discarded item grimacing at the pull it caused to his back. He rose up slowly, letting out a long breath.

When he looked to the doorway, he noted that Glynis watched him for a moment and then disappeared inside.

CHAPTER TWENTY

THE AROMA THAT wafted up to the sitting room made Glynis' stomach grumble. When Agnes announced that last meal was to be served, she hesitated about whether to go to the dining room or not.

After his last visit, she'd promised herself not to change her routine when Caelan came for a day or two. He would not have the power over her that she'd allowed before. It was best to be strong because over time it would be easier to be around her child's father.

After all, she would remain with Clan Ross and he would be an integral part of the bairn's life. The sooner she became accustomed to his presence, the better.

She stood and put down her knitting. It was the third blanket she'd made for the babe and she planned to make several more pieces. Her aunt had taught her to wash linens several times to make the fabric soft enough to make dresses for the bairn. She'd also planned to ensure to have enough nappies and such.

The corner of her bedchamber had a basket filled to the brim with different things she and her aunt had made. Her lips curved as she walked out, only for her smile to falter at seeing Caelan.

"I came to escort ye to last meal."

His newly washed hair was brushed back from his face. He'd shaven and was dressed as impeccably as always.

When her heart skipped several beats and something fluttered in her stomach, she almost whirled around and went back inside the sitting room.

Instead, she forced a blank expression and turned to walk down the corridor. Thankfully, he did not make to touch her. Instead, he fell in step and walked alongside.

"How do ye feel?"

Glynis rolled her eyes. "I am well."

"The bairn?"

"Everything is fine."

They continued to the end of the corridor, turned left, and then went down the stairs. It was at the top that he took her elbow to assist her down. Glynis almost snatched it out of his grasp but allowed it until her foot touched the ground floor. It was then she removed her arm from him and hurried to walk ahead of him toward the dining room.

"WHAT IS THAT?" Glynis sat up in bed the next morning when Agnes walked in with a tray that held a bowl and a small pitcher.

"Mister Caelan said ye liked warm bread pudding with cream." Agnes placed the tray on the side table and helped her to sit up.

Glynis pulled pillows behind her back and Agnes placed the tray on her legs and poured the cream over the hot pudding.

Her mouth watered and as much as she wanted to return the offering, Glynis could not bring herself to do it.

"Thank ye," she said meeting Agnes' gaze. "Did he speak to ye directly?"

Agnes nodded and smiled. "He came to my room and knocked. Apologized for bothering me and then asked if I could bring ye this."

"Greer must have gotten up very early to make it."

"I suppose," Agnes said with a shrug. "She and Mister Caelan are often sitting in the kitchen early mornings drinking tea together."

Reluctantly, Glynis tasted the offering. It was mouthwateringly delicious. Greer was an amazing cook.

As she finished her dessert, there was another knock on the door, and she let out a sigh. "Enter."

This time it was a different maid. She brought a beautiful cloak and hung it in the wardrobe. "Mister Caelan said to ensure ye knew he had it made for ye." The girl practically ran from the room. No doubt, Caelan told her to leave immediately so Glynis wouldn't force her to take it back.

She studied the cloak. It had a fur-lined hood and was made of a thick green wool. It was indeed beautiful. Once again, she was reluctant to return it as it would come in handy when she moved to live with Cait and Stuart where the weather was a bit colder.

Moments later Agnes returned. "Are ye ready to get up?" The maid stopped and gawked at the cloak. She walked to it and slid her hand over it. "This is beautiful."

After dressing, Glynis walked by the sitting room where her aunt and Isobel were. They'd obviously not gone down for first meal yet.

"There ye are," her aunt said. "I am famished but was waiting for ye."

"Why?" Glynis asked. "Ye did not have to."

Her aunt smiled. "It is the first day of Hogmanay, we should go down together."

They went down the stairwell to find that the great room had been decorated. The floors and tables had been thoroughly scrubbed and gleamed. There were sprigs of evergreen branches in pictures on the tables and sprays over the doorways and mantels.

The smell of mincemeat pies filled the air with spice and sweetness. Every seat was filled by guardsmen and local clan people.

The festive air made Glynis smile as Cait stood proudly with Catriona at the large round table where the women usually sat.

She dared not look to the highboard until passing. At it sat Darach, looking every bit the laird, flanking him were Ewan and Stuart. Caelan sat on Stuart's right side and Gideon at the end.

Just as they sat and were served, there was a loud bang at the front door.

Everyone clapped when Duncan walked in holding up the traditional offerings of First Footing. Which were a coin, coal, bread and a wee dram of whisky.

The handsome man grinned when a woman tugged at his tunic, and he gifted her with the shortbread.

Once again everyone clapped, and he went to the highboard and sat at the end seat.

Beatrice and the newborn were ushered through the back entrance and sat in a comfortable chair in front of one of the fireplaces that flanked both sides of the great room.

Dressed in full regalia, the brothers stood and held up tankards. Each of them wished everyone good tidings for the new year.

Glynis could not tear her eyes away from Caelan, who listened to each of his brothers speak. But unlike the others, he never smiled. Dressed in the Ross tartan that wrapped around his body, he looked every bit a Scot. His hair was shorter than his brothers, but it did not detract from the fact he was part of the family.

When his turn came, he held up his tankard and spoke in Gaelic with a strong Scottish bur. "*Lang may yer lum reek!*" Everyone laughed and clapped, lifting their drinks to repeat the words. "Long may our chimney smoke."

She had to admit, the accent did not suit him. He was, who he was. A man raised in the lowlands, but every bit a Ross.

The food was plentiful and after eating their fill, she and the other women migrated to the sitting area where Beatrice was.

Beatrice pointed to a basket. "One for each of ye." She'd brought beautifully embroidered drawstring bags as gifts.

"I will treasure it always," Glynis said holding hers against her chest.

Her aunt smiled widely as she passed out her gifts. They were ornate trinket boxes.

"I had Gideon purchase them from a ship when he traveled to his lands. He did well in choosing them."

Glynis gave handkerchiefs she'd embroidered, and everyone loved them. Isobel gifted them all with hair combs, and Cait beautifully weaved baskets. By the time they finished the gift exchange, she was glad for the basket in which to carry everything.

"This is only the first day and I am so very overwhelmed with joy," her aunt exclaimed.

IN THE AFTERNOON, after spending all morning with the women, listening to music and watching people play games, Glynis decided to rest.

As her gift, Lady Macdonald had recruited some of the women to meet in the room next to the kitchen to make mulled wine and spiced cakes. Glynis begged out feeling a bit tired.

When she turned walked down the corridor, there were footsteps behind her. She didn't have to look to know it was Caelan.

"Ye look beautiful today," he said, falling in step beside her. "Do ye need anything?"

Unsure what to say, she looked to him. "No, thank ye."

"I hope ye liked the cloak." He looked rested and content, which for some reason annoyed her.

"Caelan, ye should rejoin everyone downstairs. I am sure Darach requires ye for something."

He shook his head. "No. I do not think so."

When they reached her doorway, he opened the door for her. She would have to brush against him to pass. Refusing to let him know it affected her in any way, she went into the room. Her shoulder brushing against his chest.

"Thank ye. I prefer to be alone and rest."

When she sat to remove her shoes, he kneeled before her and unlaced them. The brush of his fingers on her ankle brought memories of their nights together.

Glynis considered kicking him away. But at the same time, she wondered what he planned to do. Curiosity got the best of her.

After he removed her shoes, he lifted his gaze to her. "I will never stop trying to win ye back, Glynis."

Bending, he pressed a soft kiss to her ankle. A handsome Scot dressed in full regalia at one's feet, pressing a kiss onto her leg was something many a lass dreamed of. Glynis was not immune.

She pressed her lips together in a tight line. "I am not sure I can ever allow ye to hurt me again like ye did. I wish it were different."

For a moment he lowered his gaze, but when he looked up, there was a challenge there. "I love ye."

The statement took her breath. Her mouth fell open and she gasped. How could he do this? Use flowery words and gestures to make her falter.

Before she could insist that he leave immediately, Caelan stood and let out a sigh. Then walked out closing the door behind.

Suddenly, a sharp pain struck in her abdomen, and she moaned, gasping at the unexpectedness of it.

The door flew open, and he raced back inside. "What happens?"

Glynis blew out several breaths. "Probably ate too much and the bairn does not like it. I am sure it is nothing to worry over."

"I will fetch my stepmother."

After the first pain, there were no more. Her aunt checked and there was no bleeding. "I am sure ye did overeat. The wee one protested. Ye should rest a bit just to be safe."

"I can stay with ye," Caelan said.

Glynis nodded. "Aye."

In truth, Glynis was scared out of her wits. What if something was wrong? It didn't matter what anyone said. She feared the worse and for some reason Caelan's presence made her feel protected.

Rain began to fall, the pattering of it on the roof and window soften the sounds of the celebrating downstairs.

Caelan looked out and then to her. "Each time it rains, I think of the cottage. I was so angry with ye."

"Ye had every right to be," Glynis agreed with a soft chuckle. "I do not know what I was thinking."

He turned and studied her. "Ye were fueled by anger. Ye wanted revenge."

"Did ye find peace after Cairn's death? Did it help?" Glynis needed to know that he no longer held anger and guilt that would twist his stomach just thinking about what the man had done to him.

"No. But it helped some."

The reply shocked her. Not just because she'd expected the opposite, but also how he'd pronounced the word. He still hated the man. The anger remained.

She wanted to see her brother's attackers pay for what they did. Only then she would find peace.

"One day yer brother will seek and find vindication. It is his battle to fight, not yers."

Once again, she was struck silent. A part of her wanted to yell to Caelan. How dare he presume to know the intricacies of what she thought and what she felt would happen?

In the recess of her mind, she realized that he was correct. It was her brother who'd fought and become disfigured. It was up to him to decide what he needed to do in response.

At the same time, how would that remove the guilt that pressed down on her?

Glynis lifted to sit. "There is no need for ye to remain. I am perfectly well. Like Aunt Mariel said. It was probably something I ate."

When Caelan nodded and left, she was quite surprised and kept watch in case the door reopened as she dressed.

When a knock came her lips curved. He was persistent. "Enter," she called out. Her mother appeared and entered; her expression expertly schooled to not show what she thought.

"Hello, Mother," Glynis said and went to kiss her mother's cheek.

Just as her lips hovered over her mother's cool check, the woman moved away removed her gray woolen cape. "I hear ye and Caelan Ross may not marry after all."

Of course, her mother was aware. Whether through correspondence with her aunt or otherwise. Glynis was not prepared to reply but had no choice.

"Ye may not be aware, but he was almost killed and has only recently recovered. I am not sure marriage is a good idea at the moment..."

It was not the first time she'd been at odds with her mother, but certainly the first to see the fury transform the otherwise pleasant face.

"Ye are with child. Unmarried and with child. Ye will marry him, and it will be soon. Yer father will speak to him immediately and ensure it. We planned to celebrate the holiday with yer brothers and family, but when I read the letter, we had to come immediately."

"Mother, it is my choice..."

Her mother closed the distance between them, her face only a sparse breath away. "Yer choice should be not to embarrass our family. Have ye not done enough to cause grief?"

In that moment, Glynis felt as if her entire world collapsed around her. Of course. Despite never stating it, her parents did hold her responsible for what happened to Gavin. If not for her recklessness, the attack that disfigured him would have never occurred.

There was nothing she could say. Instead, she nodded and scant seconds later the door slammed.

THE MUSIC THAT night sounded hollow and brought Glynis no joy. Pretending to enjoy herself as to not affect the enjoyment of the others, was tiring. But she was determined that no one would know the pain that simmered in her.

"It is lovely," she told Catriona as she sniffed the perfumed oil gift. "I will treasure it."

Surrounded by the women of Clan Ross, she felt completely protected from the outside world.

Thankfully, her mother sat at another table with Lady Macdonald, her aunt, and the visiting couple, Angus Ross and his wife. Angus Ross was younger brother to the late laird. He had a stern demeanor, but when she'd been introduced, he'd surprised her with a warm smile.

She looked past them to the other side of the room where Gideon and Caelan sat with the other men, including her father. By his relaxed countenance, she guessed her father had not spoken to him.

"Ye are quiet today," Cait said patting her hand.

"I was just thinking about what comes tomorrow. More feasting?" She pretended to be excited. "It is lovely and tiring at the same time."

Cait giggled. "That is why I escape and go for a walk. Mother and I sneak out every day."

"That is a good idea." Across the room Caelan stood and walked toward them. She held her breath and prayed he'd continue past. He did not. Instead, he stopped and looked down at yer.

"A word?"

The women stopped whatever they did to look at them. Feeling without any options, Glynis stood and allowed him to guide her toward the parlor. Once there, they went inside. It was a beautiful room, one of her favorites in the house. With large windows that afforded a view of the inlet, with the background of craggy mountainside, it was breathtaking scenery.

"Is something wrong?" she asked, glancing to him before once again directing her gaze out.

"How are ye feeling?" The question didn't surprise her. Despite their differences, he was a natural protector. And yet the questions angered her.

"Ye never inquired about my well-being at yer house."

"Gara gave me daily reports."

It occurred to her that Gara had always sought her out. Ensured she ate, made special soups for her, and desserts that the others did not get. Had it been because Caelan ordered it?

He waited for a reply and she sighed.

"I feel…"

How did she feel? There had been an odd sensation in her abdomen since the pains. But she could not say it was something wrong. It was her first pregnancy and she'd planned to ask her aunt about it.

"Glynis?" He lifted her face and looked into her eyes. "Are ye unwell?" Fear emanated from him and at the same time strength.

Glynis collapsed against him, pushing her face into his shoulder. "I do not know how I feel. It makes little sense I know." Her voice was muffled, but she didn't have the strength to move away.

"I am sure all is well. Ye could speak to yer mother or my stepmother about it." He wrapped his arms around her, and Glynis wanted to sag with relief. She'd wanted the reassurance that came from someone holding her and speaking words of comfort.

"What if something is horribly wrong? If I harmed the bairn?"

His chuckle was a deep rumble in her ear. "I am sure ye have not done anything to harm the bairn. Ye have behaved perfectly."

"I am still angry with ye." Glynis turned her head but did not lift it from his shoulder. "Ye were very unfair to me."

When his lips pressed against her temple, lingering, Glynis closed her eyes. To be in his arms, against his chest, and to have the feel of his lips again sent waves of desire through her so strong Glynis shivered.

"Are ye cold?" he asked pulling her closer.

"No." Glynis let out a long breath and pushed away. "What did ye wish to speak to me about?"

For a long moment, it was as if he would not reply. With the stance of a proud man, his gaze lingered on hers and then traveled to her lips. "I wish to discuss marriage. Glynis, I beg ye not to allow my bairn to be born out of wedlock. Marry me and I will fight to regain yer trust and caring."

"I will marry ye."

The statement made his eyes widen. He'd not expected it, but instead more angry accusations and refusal. Glynis had to marry him and not cause any more damage to the relationship with her parents.

"Mother spoke to me this morning and insisted we marry. Father will undoubtedly speak to ye about it. I say we beat them to it and announce our engagement."

"Is that why ye accepted so readily?" His expression was incredulous, angry even. "Ye do not care for me, do ye Glynis? And will do whatever it takes to ensure to keep me at arm's length."

"If ye recall sir, I was just in yer arms." Glynis glared up at him. "Why are ye angry? I just agreed to marry ye despite yer being an annoying oaf."

"I tried to protect ye."

"Ye were protecting yerself." Glynis couldn't help raising her voice.

"I will be a good father and husband," he stated emphatically, his expression filled with fury. She almost laughed at his tone.

"That ye will be a good father I do not doubt. A good husband, that is doubtful."

He leaned over until their noses almost touched. "I love ye woman. Why would I not be a good husband?"

"Because ye are…maddening."

When his mouth covered hers, Glynis almost cried with joy. She desired him so much in that moment that she'd considered throwing herself against him.

His lips took hers with the same desperation she felt, and Glynis reacted by wrapping her arms around his neck and pulling him closer.

Kissing, licking, and trailing his tongue down the side of her neck to the top of her bosom, Caelan seemed to know exactly what she needed. He guided her to a chaise, and they fell upon it. Him over her.

His weight felt perfect.

"I have missed ye," Glynis admitted kissing his jaw and pressing kisses to his throat. "So much."

Caelan hummed. "Me or my body?"

"Both," Glynis admitted.

They had little privacy, anyone could happen upon them, but somehow that fanned the flames of her heated need.

Pushing her skirts up, Caelan nestled between her legs and lowered the front of his breeches. He then lifted his sex from the confines.

Glynis reached between them to touch him and wrapped her fingers around his staff.

"Ahh!" Caelan moaned into her ear sending tendrils of heat down her body to the very center.

There was no thinking involved, but only the voluntary want of two people overwhelmed with need.

She guided him between her legs, and he did not hesitate to thrust into her. When she cried out, he covered her mouth with his. Then without breaking the kiss, he drove in and out, faster and faster. Both rushing to reach release.

With each movement, Glynis wanted to cry out, but she held it in which in a way made the experience more enjoyable. The length of his hardness pushed deep, while his girth stretched her to a point that nearly caused her to lose control.

They fit perfectly together, his masculine body over her more languid softer one.

"Yes," Glynis whispered as everything spiraled and her hold on reality began to slip. "Oh, yes."

Caelan drove harder, as he too seemed to lose control.

When she found release, her entire body went rigid, and her toes curled. At the same time, Caelan pushed his mouth into her hair, his muffled moan sending trickles of desire through her.

"Goodness," Glynis said practically shoving him off. "Someone could have happened upon us."

With a wicked grin, he straightened, adjusted himself, and held out his hand to help her up when she finished fumbling with her skirts.

The sound of a throat clearing made Caelan spin around to see who'd walked in. With purposeful steps, Gideon came into view.

There was no doubt in Glynis' mind the man knew what had just occurred. And yet, his face was a mask without emotion.

"Mother sent me to find ye," he said looking at Caelan. "It seems yer parents have requested to speak to both of ye," he added looking at Glynis.

Making the statement, he turned and walked out.

"Do ye think he saw us?" Glynis asked, her cheeks burning.

"I think he heard," Caelan replied, then scanned her from head to toe. "We should go see what they wish to speak to us about.

They walked through the great hall and into the dining room. The family was gathering there for meals to seek solace from the overfilled great hall.

When they walked in, not only were her parents there, but also Darach and Isobel as well as her Aunt Mariel.

"Before anyone says anything, may I speak?" Caelan inquired. At the silence, he continued.

"Glynis and I have come to an agreement and wish to marry immediately. I will not allow my bairn to be born out of wedlock."

Her father jumped up. "And well ye should marry her." His bravado was lost since he'd obviously been prepared for her or Caelan not wishing to marry.

"Father, we will get married." Glynis wasn't sure why she clarified, but the silence after her father's statement had felt awkward.

Her aunt gleamed. "There will be a wedding in the morning. How delightful to have a wedding during Hogmanay." She grinned at Glynis and then Isobel clapped, obviously as excited as Lady Mariel.

Her mother's smile didn't quite reach her eyes and Glynis knew she was still disappointed.

CHAPTER TWENTY-ONE

After an evening of feasting and revelry, Caelan slept deeply. He ordered a hot bath upon waking, needing to ease the stiffness that continued to assault his back.

It was to be his wedding day and despite the gloomy sunless morning, he was in good spirits.

Just then Bram entered. "Mister Caelan, do ye require anything?"

It was only a week since he'd hired the young man to be his squire and so far, he'd proven to be a good choice.

"Go see if Miss Glynis' maid has retrieved the item, I had Greer cook for her."

The young man hurried out as he lowered into the hot water.

It was his habit to rise early. He enjoyed the peaceful silence of the morning, just before everyone woke and the activities of the household began.

He was dressing when there was a hurried knock on the door. When he called to whoever it was to enter, he was surprised to see Agnes.

"Mister Caelan," the woman said, her face pale. "Ladies Ross are with Miss Glynis. She is unwell—"

He did not let her finish, rounding her and racing to Glynis' bedchamber. He pushed the door open and immediately knew something was horribly wrong. The smell of blood filled the air and Glynis moaned and then sobbed.

"Oh, dear," his stepmother said upon seeing him. "Ye must go. Leave at once." She hurried to him pushing him out the open door. "Do not reenter. I will speak to ye as soon as this is over."

"Over?" He knew what happened, but his mind would not accept it. "The bairn?"

His stepmother closed her eyes and waved to a woman who arrived to enter.

"Who is she?" he asked.

"A midwife. The bairn arrives." His stepmother met his gaze. "Go find her mother. Please."

He mentally calculated how far along Glynis was. If she'd become with child the first time, they'd been together, it was only nearing four months. Not long enough to ensure the wee one would survive.

Somehow, he managed to find out where Glynis' parents were, but by the way her mother rushed past him, she'd gotten the news from someone else.

Instead of returning upstairs, he slumped into the nearest chair to await news.

He wasn't sure how long it was before his worst fears were confirmed. Darach guided him into the parlor, where his other brothers joined them.

"The bairn was a boy. He did not survive."

When Caelan attempted to leave, they blocked his exit.

"There is more," Darach said, his face stoic. "Glynis' life is in peril. She is losing blood."

He didn't allow anyone to block his way as he raced

through the corridors until bursting into the room.

The women in the room looked to him, but no one made to stop him. Caelan rounded the bed, ignoring the glare from the midwife who was stuffing a cloth between Glynis' legs.

She was pale, but awake. Her eyes widening at seeing him.

"Son . . ." his stepmother began, but stopped talking when Glynis held out her arms to him. He closed the distance and hugged her to him, allowing her to cry softly. "I lost the bairn. What will happen now? The poor, poor wee one."

She kept repeating questions, not waiting for a reply and he remained steadfast whispering encouragements into her ear.

"The bleeding is stopping," someone said.

"Thank God," Glynis' mother replied sniffing loudly.

The room was cleaned up by silent maids and a window opened to allow for fresh air. Then one by one everyone left.

Glynis slept, her hand clutched in his. Caelan feared that she'd lost too much blood and would perish at any moment, so he refused to leave her side even when first her parents came for a while, and then his stepmother.

It was late when Glynis awakened, her swollen eyes meeting his. "Where is he?"

He looked to his stepmother, who shook her head.

"He is bundled and will be buried in the morning. Ye can watch from here." She pointed to the small window.

A maid entered with broth and bread. After prodding, Glynis ate most of it. Her gaze kept moving to the window and Caelan knew she thought of the child.

"CAELAN?"

He woke with a start, his aching neck, from falling asleep in a chair, made him grimace. Glynis studied him, her gaze clear. "Ye should go to bed. I am fine."

"I will not leave ye."

"I'd prefer it."

The words stung, but Caelan ignored it. He would not allow her to use words to push him away.

UNFORTUNATELY, THREE DAYS later, when he went to check on her, Glynis was gone.

There was a letter on the table next to the bed with his name on it.

Dearest Caelan,

I have returned to Barra with my parents.

It is time for me to take responsibility for so many things. I must face my fears and only then can I be what someone like ye needs.

Dare I hope that ye will wait for me?

Glynis.

He crumpled the letter and with it in his fist, he rushed out and down the stairs. When he saw his stepmother, she looked at him with alarm. "What is the matter?"

"Did ye know Glynis was to return with her parents?"

"Glynis is gone?" Her eyes widened. "No, I did not."

BARRA GREETED HER with rain and gloom. It matched how she

felt. It had been horrible of her to leave without telling anyone. She'd not even told her parents, instead stealing into the carriage before them and surprising them when they'd climbed into it.

"Ye should say something," her mother had scolded. But upon her adamant refusal, she had relented as they were anxious to return to Barra.

"What do ye plan to do Glynis?" her mother asked as the familiar surroundings of her village came into view. "Nothing reckless, I hope."

She met her father's gaze. "I plan to rest and get my strength. Then I will help with the household."

Her parents exchanged a strange look.

"What is it? Am I not welcome at my own home?"

"Of course, ye are welcome. It is yer home," her mother said. "However, there have been some changes. Despite the bairn not surviving. Ye are betrothed."

Her father frowned. "The young man seems honorable. Stood by ye for days. Why are ye running from him?"

"I am not running from him. I need to ensure things are made right between Gavin and myself. I must ensure the attackers pay for—"

"That is not yer fight," her father interrupted slashing his hand across. "Ye must not interfere in what is Gavin's right to see about."

The air in the carriage seemed to lessen, but Glynis took a deep breath despite it. "It was all my fault."

Her father took her hand. "It was all the fault of the men who attacked ye and yer brother. None of the burden should be on ye." His gaze was gentle as it moved from her to her mother. "Stop blaming yerself."

It was as if the last of the air was sucked out of the carriage and Glynis fell back and closed her eyes. Later she would sob with the relief that came from her father's words. It was as if the burden she'd carried was lifted and her entire body felt light.

When she opened her eyes, her father smiled at her. "And when Caelan Ross comes for ye, I do not want any argument. Ye will marry him."

The carriage came to a stop and they climbed down assisted by her brother, Gavin, who smiled warmly at her.

The scarring seemed less prominent than she remembered. Yes, there was the cut across the side of his face, but it wasn't as horrible as before she'd left. When she examined his face, she realized that while Gavin was as handsome as before, somehow the scar gave him a roguish appeal.

"Not sure what to think of yer study of me," he said frowning. "Have ye missed my façade that much?"

Glynis laughed and allowed his tight hug.

"I did not expect ye," Gavin said. "What are ye planning to do?"

"A wedding," her mother interjected. "We must plan for a wedding. It will be within a day or two at the most."

TWO DAYS LATER, Glynis stood in the front of the small chapel in the nearby village and exchanged vows with a very handsome man she had no doubt loved her.

Caelan stood tall and proud, his wide shoulders touching hers as they repeated after the clergy. Next to him stood Gideon, who'd barely made it in time after disappearing into the village, no doubt at the invitation of one of the local women.

Dressed in a lavender gown with flowers in her hair, Glynis felt beautiful. Upon meeting her new husband's gaze there was little doubt she was in fact the luckiest woman in the world.

That night after a huge meal, they went into the bedchamber that used to be hers alone.

Glynis felt shy when undressing. She could not fully undress as she still bled from the miscarriage. But she donned a nightdress and slipped into the bed.

"I suppose we will not be able to have a proper wedding night for a bit." She did her best to put on a brave front, but any reminder of the loss of her child made her tear up immediately.

Caelan seemed not to notice. "I do not mind. What is important to me is that ye recover fully. There is no hurry." He leaned over and pressed a kiss to her lips.

It was to be the first of many nights they'd spend together. She anticipated his warm skin against hers. But Caelan did not undress fully either and wore a soft tunic to bed.

The weather was cold, so it made sense, but there was a nagging feeling something else was wrong.

"Do ye always sleep with a tunic on?"

"It is quite cold in here."

She lifted to look at the fire in the hearth. "Add a log."

"I am fine."

"Is it because ye do not wish for me to see yer back?"

Caelan turned to his side and gazed at her. The glow of the fire made him look like a marble statue of a god. With perfect slashes for eyebrows, long lashes, and a well-formed mouth, an artist would be hard-pressed to duplicate his features well.

"I am not comfortable for ye to see my scars. Although I am aware it will not change how ye feel. They may be repelling."

She doubted it, but decided not to push him. He would undress fully when he was ready.

They would not make love that night, her body still recovering, however, holding each other as they fell asleep was just as intimate a moment.

A LOUD SNIFF woke her the next morning. She opened her eyes and at first did not see anything. Caelan had obviously gotten up to place a new log into the fire because it burned brightly.

He stood halfway turned with something in his hands. It was one of the wee one's blankets that she'd knitted. Glynis had kept one and left the rest behind. Not that she needed a reminder of the bairn, but more that she needed something physical that she could hold.

Caelan had stood next to her, watching as they'd buried the bairn. Both her parents and her aunt surrounded by the rest of the Ross family had stood in the rain as the tiny box had been placed into the ground.

Glynis squeezed her eyes shut and then opened them to study Caelan. He grieved in silence, head bent and wide shoulders shuddering. Unable to not comfort him, she slid from the bed and went to him.

"I know," she said, and they held each other until the waves of grief passed and allowed them to return to bed.

CHAPTER TWENTY-TWO

Spring 1604

GLYNIS PEERED OUT the carriage door and didn't recognize any of the passing terrain. "Where are we?"

"Heading west. We are about two or three hours from where Stuart and Cait live." Caelan leaned back and closed his eyes.

She gave up trying to talk to him about this unexpected trip. In the months of knowing him, it became clear that once he made up his mind about something, Caelan could not be persuaded otherwise.

A long while later, when Caelan opened his eyes, she smiled at him. "Are we to visit Cait and Stuart?"

He slid closer and peered out. "Perhaps. Ah, yes, almost there."

In the four months since they'd married. They lived at her parent's home for a month. Once her body felt back to normal, they returned to Caelan's house, where they'd remained for three months. Caelan continued to keep the clan ledgers, while training an apprentice. Now he'd claimed it was time for them to go on a trip. Before she could have a say in the matter, they traveled to the east coast of South Uist.

After the first few hours of the familiar route, they'd turned and taken a route that seemed different to Glynis than when they'd visited Cait and Stuart previously, but she wasn't well acquainted enough with the area to know for sure.

She nudged Caelan's shoulder and peered up at him. "Are ye glad to have married me?"

Leaning to the side, he rested his head on hers. "If ye do not believe it by now, then I have not been pleasing ye enough."

"Oh, ye have not failed when it comes to lovemaking."

Tipping her face up, he peered into her eyes. "I love ye, Glynis, and am fortunate to have ye for a wife."

Despite how many times Caelan repeated how he felt, it was surreal to her. "I am the fortunate one. Ye are the most beautiful man I have ever met. I love that ye do not stand in my way when I wish to do things but give guidance instead. With ye I have become less impulsive, I believe."

His brow lifted. "Like when ye and Beatrice hid in the bushes and spied on Duncan and I when we bathed in the loch?"

Glynis' felt her eyes widen. "Ye know about that?"

Just then the driver knocked on the carriage and Caelan stuck his head out and said something. Glynis slid to peer out, but Caelan took the opportunity to lift her onto his lap and took her mouth with his.

A tryst in the carriage would have been delightful, but Glynis was aware they'd slowed to a crawl. As adventurous as she was, it would not do for one of Stuart's men to catch them in the act.

"Stop, Caelan. We are obviously almost there." She pinched his bottom lip between her teeth. "I promise to make it up to ye later."

His low growl made her tingle with excitement. Her husband knew exactly how to make her forget everything.

The driver knocked again and Caelan opened the carriage door.

"What a beautiful view," Glynis said catching sight of the sea in the distance. When she turned, her mouth fell open and tears immediately burned her eyes.

It was the cottage. The ugly cottage where they'd first made love. But it was very different now. Some of the same frame remained, but it was larger now. The stables to the side of it had been rebuilt and were now a bit further from the home. There was a corral with two horses, cows grazing nearby, and a smaller pen with goats.

She stood silent taking it all in, her gaze returning to the house. It reminded her of the house Stuart and Cait lived in, with a beautiful front door and large windows that would afford views of the sea. Craning her neck, she realized a second floor had been added, along with a balcony from which one could stand and enjoy the view.

"Oh, goodness," she said and took off at a run toward the house. Just before she entered, Caelan scooped her up into his arms and together they crossed the threshold to the inside.

It was furnished beautifully. Glynis immediately recognized Caelan's tastes in dark woods and thick rugs.

"It is breathtaking," she exclaimed. "Put me down so I can explore." When he did, she rushed from one room to the next, her smile so wide that after a while, her face ached.

"Caelan, how did ye do it?"

He gave her a sheepish grin. "When I told ye I was going to patrol with my brothers, this is where we went. A large group of the guards and some men from the village worked tirelessly to complete it."

There were voices outside and she hurried to the door and then outside.

Cait waived with enthusiasm. "I am so glad we are to be close to one another." She frowned at her husband who greeted Caelan with a hug. "Stuart, help me down."

It was comical to watch Cait attempt to climb down from the carriage when so heavy with child.

"Ye should not have come. Ye are much too close to the bairn's birth to be out," Glynis chided, but it was accompanied with a happy smile and hug. "Have ye seen it inside?"

Cait shook her head. "No, this is the first time I've come here. It is beautiful." They walked into the house arm in arm, behind them Clara and Cait's companion, Cora.

They'd brought food, so before long everyone sat around the dining table and enjoyed the first meal at the house.

"Clara, I hope ye can accompany me to the village to shop for necessities," Glynis inquired of Cait's mother. "We do not have servants. I suppose that is another thing we need. Someone to help me. I do not require more than one or two at the most."

Caelan gave her a knowing look. "Agnes is coming to live here, she and Bram will arrive in a few days. If ye wish to hire a chambermaid, then ye should find someone from the village who can go home daily."

"How far is it?" she asked.

"I thought ye were here before," Cait said.

When Caelan cleared his throat and Glynis' cheeks turned red, Cait laughed. "Ye did not see much I take it?"

"It was raining quite hard," Glynis replied giving Caelan a warning look, not to elaborate.

"The village is within walking distance," Caelan said. "Ye can visit often with Bree."

Glynis had never felt so happy in her life. She sighed and glanced at Caelan. "I have so many questions and yet this is the happiest day of my life."

When Stuart burst out laughing, Glynis realized she'd not considered her wedding day. "Next to our wedding day, of course."

"Of course," everyone repeated, while chuckling. Glynis gave up and joined them.

There were loud bangs at the door and both Stuart and Caelan immediately got to their feet. The door opened and Artair walked in.

"Why wasn't I invited?"

The brothers exchanged looks. Stuart shook his head. "Because I did not know ye were back."

"Where were ye?" Caelan asked.

Artair shrugged. "On patrol. I found a family living south of here. Trouble."

"Oh, no," Cait said. "Do not tell me. Another encroacher bent on no good?"

Everyone waited until finally Artair replied. "A young lad stole my clothes. I had to ride naked to find where he lived. The mother did not bat an eye when I demanded my clothing back. Instead, she practically ran me off."

Both Stuart and Caelan fought to keep from laughing by pressing their lips into tight lines.

"How could she run ye off?" Cait asked, her eyes wide.

Artair narrowed his eyes at his cousins. "I did manage to reclaim my bow and quiver, but she claimed not to have my sword."

Everyone was silent. Then Stuart blew out a breath. "Is she a beauty?"

"Aye."

"Husband?" Caelan asked.

Artair shrugged. "I really liked that sword."

THAT NIGHT, THEY made love and fell exhausted onto the bedding, their chests heaving as they tried to regain control of their breathing.

"Thank ye," Glynis said and rolled to her side to press a kiss onto Caelan's jaw.

"Of course," Caelan said. "I can repeat it nightly."

Glynis giggled. "Not that. Thank ye for the house, for being so thoughtful."

"It is I who will never tire of showing ye how grateful I am that ye forgave me. I was wrong to push ye away and vow never to do so again."

She snuggled against him, her head on his shoulder. "I love ye, Caelan Ross. Even though ye are more English than Scot."

"I never lived in England. I was schooled in Glasgow, which is in Scotland."

"Are ye sure?" She lifted her head and studied him. "Ye seem so English."

He rolled her onto her back. "Be silent wench," he pronounced in a deep bur. "Or I will have my way with ye."

Her laughter filled the room.

CHAPTER TWENTY-THREE

"I THOUGHT YE were to stay here longer," Stuart said giving Artair a pointed look. "Why are ye leaving so soon?"

Artair let out a breath. "Ye no longer require my help. There is little for me to do here. I have gotten plenty of rest and ate so much my breeches are getting tight.

His cousin burst out laughing. "If ye are broader, tis cause ye visit Dougal and Bree, hoping to have her meat pies."

"Aye they are quite good," Artair replied with a grin. "It is best I be on my way. I must check on my father and return to my duties for Darach. It is time that I take my turn at the southern guard post."

By the look in Stuart's face, he too missed being a guard. However, his cousin had his hands full between overseeing the lands and the nearby village people who saw him as laird.

"Thank ye for all yer help cousin."

TWO DAYS LATER Artair rode toward the keep and dismounted to stretch his legs. His injured leg continued to bother him, and he wondered if he'd be able to ride once older.

Probably not.

The sounds of a gurgling nearby creek beckoned and he guided his horse to the water's edge. Lowering to the ground, he drank of the cool water.

At the sound of rustling leaves, he jerked up and looked around. A short distance away, a timid doe came from the foliage and drank from the water seeming not to feel threatened by him.

Artair watched it for a long time until the wind shifted, and she caught his sent. Immediately her heard lifted and she looked at him. Then quick as the wind she darted away.

A soft chuckle escaped, and he looked to his horse. "Reminds me of someone we recently met. Ye recall, the woman whose child stole my clothes."

The horse of course, did not reply.

"Aye she is a beauty. Large brown eyes, like those of the doe there," he continued motioning to where the animal had just gone.

"A rare beauty."

At the memory, Artair let out a breath. It was probably the woman he'd met was married, which suited him just fine as he planned to never marry. Marriage was too constricting for a nomad like him.

The Stag

The Stag: Artair's story, is the next one in the Clan Ross of the Hebrides series.

Everything about Artair Ross's life is about to change. Cousin to the Laird and proud member of the warrior force, he is forced to give it all up to take over his ailing father's duties. However, when attackers overtake a village, he is guarding, a shipwreck occurs and a horrible family tragedy happens, it is more than apparent Artair is in for greater battles than he's ever known.

Robena Mackay is devastated when her son is ripped away by her late husband's family. After losing her parents and now her only child, she decides to fight back with all the strength she has left. Despite being a proud independent woman, when the laird's cousin insists on becoming her defender, she pushes pride aside. Afterall, the assistance of a handsome protector may be her only option in the struggle that has become her life.

Will love soften the harshness of tragedy and loss?

ABOUT THE AUTHOR

Enticing. Engaging. Romance.

USA Today Bestselling Author Hildie McQueen writes strong brooding alphas who meet their match in feisty brave heroines. If you like stories with a mixture of passion, drama, and humor, you will love Hildie's storytelling where love wins every single time!

A fan of all things pink, Paris, and four-legged creatures, Hildie resides in eastern Georgia, USA, with her super-hero husband Kurt and three little yappy dogs.

Join my reader group on Facebook: bit.ly/31YCee1
Sign up for my newsletter and get a free book! goo.gl/jLzPTA
Visit her website at www.hildiemcqueen.com
Facebook: facebook.com/HildieMcQueen
Twitter: twitter.com/authorhildie
Instagram instagram.com/hildiemcqueenwriter

Made in the USA
Columbia, SC
25 May 2022